THE ISLANDS OF ALARISS

CHAPTER I

RAGING WATERS

Quinn stood on the ship's foredeck while the storm raged all around him. Lightning crashed through the sky, splitting the clouds and flickering white light across the dark waves. Rain lashed into his face. Every time the ship was driven into the mountainous waves the impact made his teeth judder, and great sheets of spray surged across the deck. His clothes were soaked through and his hands were freezing where he gripped the wooden rail.

He'd been on the merchant ship, the *Seagull*, for two days now, ploughing his way through the storms that plagued the seas between Yaross and Keriss Islands. The days and nights merged into one now that summer had turned into a brutal, storm-laden autumn, and everything was shrouded in fog. But despite the rough conditions, Quinn preferred it up on deck.

'Damn it!' he cursed, dodging another wave that came crashing over his feet, soaking his legs. A voice called from above him as he grabbed onto the rigging.

'You, boy!' the voice growled. 'Get below deck!'

Quinn could just make out the shadowy figure of the captain's mate, high in his crow's nest. Quinn mouthed a reply to suggest he couldn't hear above the shrieking of the rain, and pulled his wind-blown hood back over his head, ignoring him. Even though Thea, his fellow runaway, and Ignus, the Dragon Knight, would be down there, all he wanted right now was the fresh air and the wind.

Just a few weeks ago he'd been an orphan living with his aunt in a tiny village on Yaross, the least important of the Twelve Islands of Alariss. It wasn't until he'd been forced to join the Black Guard trainees and he discovered he had dragon-blood – with the power to morph from a human into a fearsome dragon – that he'd had to run away.

Quinn had grown up believing that the Dragon Knights had betrayed the Imperial Family and murdered them; but it was all a big lie. His aunt, Marta, had shown him the truth. The person who had really murdered the Emperor and Empress was Vayn, the Emperor's own brother. And even more difficult to believe, the Emperor and Empress were his parents and he, Quinn, was now the true Emperor.

Lightning flashed again, casting pink and purple forks of electricity pulsing across the sky. Quinn flinched and wrapped his cloak more tightly around him, gripping the wooden railing until his knuckles turned white. He heard the captain's mate hollering again from above.

Back in Yaross Quinn and Thea had managed to escape the Black Guard and use Quinn's magical sword to free the first of the Dragon

Knights, Ignus, the Flame Dragon. Together they had helped to free Ignus's village from the Black Guard's tyranny, but Emperor Vayn had discovered what they'd done all too quickly.

That was why Quinn, Ignus and Thea had to bribe their way onto the *Seagull*: they were keeping a low profile until they were strong enough to face Vayn. Now Quinn spent his days deep in thought, Ignus made friends with the rowdy sailors and Thea practised her magic spells in a quiet corner.

The storm winds thrummed madly through the ship's rigging, battering the creaking vessel into the gigantic waves. The clouds above were black as the gods' rage.

'Quinn?' a voice shouted through the howl of the storm.

Quinn turned, half-expecting to see the grizzled face of an angry sailor. Instead, blinking the rain out of her eyes, Thea was staggering up from below deck and clutching on to a line. She tried to shield herself from the whipping rain, her bright red hair clinging to her face as she struggled to find her feet.

'What are you doing up here?' she shouted.

Quinn reached out for her as she traversed the slippery deck. 'I'm thinking,' he called.

'Try thinking down below, you idiot!' Thea shrieked, stretching for his fingertips. 'There's less chance of being struck by lightning!'

Thea grabbed out towards Quinn and hauled herself up beside him, against the angle of the towering waves.

'And more chance of losing my temper with those sailors . . .' Quinn replied. Earlier, Quinn and Thea had been playing cards with the sailors below deck, but the cheating captain had got the fiery dragonblood coursing through Quinn's veins once more. It was only a game, but Quinn couldn't control it. It was a good job all he could muster was a golden talon or two. If he'd turned into a dragon the size of Ignus, the whole ship would have gone down.

'Dragonform getting to you?' Thea asked. 'It'll just take time – my magic didn't come over-night . . .'

'It's not just that,' Quinn shrugged awkwardly,

although he did wish he had more control over his dragon abilities. 'It's my parents.' He peered out over the rail at the heaving, dark water. Wind thrashed the top of the waves into foamy white crests and sent spray lashing through the air. 'This is where they drowned – just off the coast of Keriss. Aunt Marta told me they were fishing . . .'

But she'd been lying, protecting him from the Black Guard. And yet it still hurt that she hadn't told him the truth. *She could have trusted me*, he thought.

'. . . But they weren't fishing,' Thea said. 'They were the Emperor and Empress.'

Quinn nodded. 'Whatever they were doing out here, they didn't just sink – Vayn must have sabotaged their ship. My father was a dragon-blood. He could have got out of there when it started to sink, but he didn't . . .' He stared gloomily into the water as it surged and fell away beneath them, raising the ship up and then dropping it down with a thump that shook the timbers. 'Their ship is still down there somewhere.'

Once again he was snapped out of his thoughts by the captain's mate barking from above.

'Land ahoy!' the sailor roared from his crow's nest. 'Beware the rocks!'

Shouts and crashes sounded across the ship. Quinn's amber eyes flashed. *Rocks?* For a moment he imagined their own ship going down in these stormy seas, the cold waves crashing over the side, the planks splitting and breaking apart and the angry water closing over them . . .

Sailors came hurrying up from the hatches and raced for the lines; some of the ropes were as thick as Quinn's arm. Ignus stamped up behind them, his face a sickly green. When he wasn't playing cards with the sailors down below trying to distract himself, he'd been curled up on his bunk. Apparently flame dragons didn't mix too well with water.

'What's happening?' Quinn shouted as Ignus stumbled up to them uneasily. For such a big, strong man, he was clearly lacking sea legs.

'We're almost at Keriss harbour,' Ignus rumbled in reply, running a hand across his stubbly chin.

'Thank the Heavens. Look.' He pointed a thick finger ahead of them.

The clouds and mist slowly began to lift, giving the voyagers a better view of where they were heading. However, what Quinn saw didn't fill him with confidence. Rocks jutted out from the waves like a dragon's talons, curving high above the ship's mast; a narrow channel snaked its way between the cliffs to clear water beyond with the port in the distance. Water whirled through the channel – it looked like a shipwreck waiting to happen.

'We make for the Kerissian Pass! All hands on deck!' the captain called, grabbing the helm from a lowly member of the crew. The rest of the sailors manned their stations, pulling at ropes and bustling around on deck.

'Are they crazy?' Thea shouted up at Ignus. 'We'll never make it through there.'

'It's the only way,' Ignus bellowed back. 'You might want to hang on. This is going to get choppy!'

The sailors eased out the sails as far as they would go as the wind came around behind them;

the ship ran before the wind, heading right for the cliffs, picking up speed. The captain seemed to be having trouble controlling its direction as they raced over the waves. Shouts and yells sounded as the sailors struggled to manage their lines. The curving talons of rock seemed to close in over the ship as it headed for the entrance to the harbour. Quinn was sure he could reach out and brush his fingers against them as the sharp rocks sliced by.

'It's not wide enough,' he groaned.

'Hang on!' Thea cried.

As if in response, a gust of wind sent their ship slipping sideways towards one of the towering rocks. Quinn yelled in surprise, but the next moment the sailors were hauling on a line, pulling a sail across, and the ship darted in the other direction.

A sudden swirl in the wind sent the sail on the port side snapping across the deck – the wooden boom splintered like a matchstick. With a yell, a sailor holding his line was sent spinning over the planks to crash into the guardrail. The line he'd been holding slashed back and forth in the air as the sail snapped loosely from the mast. Immediately, the ship lost speed and began to drift, driven by the running waves.

Quinn and Thea stared in horror as the ship lurched directly towards a jagged spike of rock that rose up from the waves like a spear.

'No!' Quinn yelled. 'It's going to crash . . .!'

CHAPTER 2
A FROSTY RECEPTION

Sailors were shouting and bellowing all around. Quinn watched as the loose sail flapped in the storm surge. His parents' ship had gone down just here. Now the *Seagull* was heading for the same rocks.

And then Vayn will have won, Quinn thought. *That's not going to happen!*

'Starboard down!' the captain shouted.

Quinn watched the rope whip back and forth, out of control. Waves broke over the deck sending water washing over the planks. The ship rocked from side to side as though shaken by an angry sea god. Quinn clenched his fists.

The rope snapped across the deck and tangled in the rail on the other side.

Now's my chance! Quinn thought, throwing himself forward.

'What are you—?' Thea yelled.

Quinn ignored her. He bounced off the foremast as the ship slipped into another trough and then wallowed back up. Water rushed over his legs – it was like trying to stand on ice. Quinn found himself slipping faster and faster towards the rail, which he hit with enough force to knock the breath out of his body. He tried to suck in air, but a wave crashed over him, filling his mouth with salty, freezing water. He spluttered it out and grabbed on tight to the rail. His lungs were desperate for air but the seawater was still swirling over his head.

Then the ship heaved, sloshing to the port side. The water rushed back off the deck as the vessel was flung in the opposite direction. Quinn gasped and blinked the stinging water out of his eyes.

There, right next to him, was the rope, lashing angrily back and forth as its sail flapped in the storm wind. Each time it snapped like a whip, the rail groaned.

Grimacing, Quinn let go of the rail and seized hold of the rope.

With a crack, the rail gave way. Without its anchor, the sail billowed out, hauling Quinn with it. He scrabbled with his feet, trying to grip the deck, but it was no good.

'Hold on!' Ignus bellowed.

'I am!' Quinn shouted as the rope sent him spinning across the deck. If he could just get it caught around the mast, he thought, then maybe he could get it under control.

The rope jerked in the opposite direction, almost pulling Quinn's arms out of their sockets. He yelled in pain.

Suddenly, an enormous hand clamped around his leg and stopped him in his tracks as Ignus seized hold of him, then Thea. The rope burned through his hands as sailors came rushing up behind him, grabbing at the rope and hauling it in. Quinn dug in and pulled, gritting his teeth.

'Lash the boom!' one of the sailors hollered, and two other sailors raced over to repair the broken wood.

Even with the sailors to help, the rope was bucking in Quinn's hands like a wild horse trying to wrench itself free. Quinn's muscles screamed, but he didn't let go.

'Bring it to port,' the sailor shouted.

Together, they fought the rope, hauling the sail over to the left side of the ship. With every step, the rope tried to pull Quinn off his feet and send him flying across the deck.

'Here,' the sailor said through gritted teeth. He whipped the end of the rope around a wooden cleat jutting from the deck and pulled it tight. The sail billowed, but the cleat held. For a moment, the howling wind dropped just enough for the ship to level out, and the *Seagull* lurched to port and away from the rocks.

Finally Quinn let go and slumped onto the deck. The sailors fell in a sprawling mass of bodies like a deck of cards.

Thea let out a high-pitched laugh of delight, as she scrambled up. 'We did it!'

Ignus rubbed his head and hauled himself up, his face grass green with nausea. 'I think I really am going to be sick now.'

Once Quinn was safe, his body shook like a leaf. But the ship was moving again. The captain was leaning into his wheel and they were coming around, further away from the rocks, picking up speed and heading once more for the gap in the cliffs.

'That was pretty stupid,' Thea hissed. 'You could have been killed!'

'We could all have been killed,' Quinn said.

Thea grabbed Quinn's hands – they were red, raw and bleeding from where the rope had sliced through them. She muttered a quick spell under her breath and Quinn felt the pain disappear as her magic healed him.

'Sails down!' the captain bellowed, and the sailors rushed to drop the remaining sails.

Quinn looked back and saw the deathly Kerissian Pass behind them fading into the distance.

He flashed a grin at Thea as the ship sailed smoothly into the calm of the harbour.

He cocked his head and gave her a cheeky smile. 'I don't know what all the fuss was about.'

Quinn, Thea and Ignus disembarked just as the sun was beginning to set, and made their way off the landing station.

'Port Keriss used to be one of the great ports of the Twelve Islands,' Ignus rumbled. 'Ships from every corner of Alariss came here to unload their cargoes. Now look at it.'

Apart from their own ship, there was only one other large boat moored in the docks. Further along, black-hulled fishing boats had been hauled up onto the stony shore and fishermen were unloading their catches. The smell of fish drifted on the breeze and small, closely packed stone houses hugged the narrow streets lining the water. It was clear the place had seen better days.

'I bet I know who's responsible,' Thea muttered.

Quinn nodded in agreement, hauling his leather satchel onto his back. Lights began coming on in the little cottages as daylight slipped away. As he passed a moored boat, he caught a glimpse of himself in one of the glass portholes. His smooth, tanned face looked weather-beaten and raw. His shoulder-length hair was tangled and in desperate need of taming.

'C'mon. We can't stay here all night,' he called, striding off the jetty.

But . . . where are we going to stay? he wondered, as he made his way onto the cobbled street.

Out of the corner of his eye he spotted a man hurrying along the dock, heading for the town. *The locals will know.*

'Hey!' Quinn called.

The man shot him a dark look.

'Hey!' Quinn tried again. 'We're looking for a hostel or an inn . . . Can you —?'

The man pulled his hood further over his eyes, muttered something under his breath, and hurried away.

'What was that about?' Quinn frowned – surely he didn't look *that* scruffy?

'It's not just him,' Thea said. 'Look.'

The locals working on their nets and boats were shooting angry looks at Quinn, Thea and Ignus and muttering to each other.

'How's that for a welcome to Keriss?' Quinn asked, sarcastically.

Quinn knew that people were often suspicious of strangers – the Black Guard made sure of that. But he'd never seen a town that was so unfriendly; he felt uncomfortable in his own skin.

'Ignore them,' Ignus growled. 'I've been here before and I know where there's a good hostel. Follow me.'

Casting another glance at the hostile groups of locals, Quinn hurried after Ignus and Thea, up the winding streets until they found themselves outside a dilapidated hostel.

Quinn looked up at the battered sign hanging from a rusty hinge. The paint was peeling so badly that he could hardly make out the picture of the Kerissian Mountains decorating it.

'*Travellers' Rest*?' Thea mocked. 'Looks lovely!'

'It wasn't like this last time I was here,' Ignus grunted, shrugging his huge shoulders. 'You're not going to find much luxury away from the capital these days. Emperor Vayn has drained people dry. But they'll still have beds . . .'

He pushed open the door and ducked inside. They found themselves in a low-ceilinged common room with a dozen tables scattered around. A smoky fire burned in a big fireplace and the air was filled with the smell of old smoke and the rotting rushes that were scattered across the floor. Quinn had to squint to look around the room as there were only a couple of guttering oil lamps on the walls to light the place.

Ignus kept his head low to avoid the heavy, cracked oak beams as he strode across to the bar. Quinn and Thea followed him. Quinn tried to ignore the hostile glances they were getting from the groups of men around the room.

'We need rooms,' Ignus said to the landlord, as he leaned over the bar.

The landlord eyed him up and down. He was

well built with a long scar across his jaw, but Ignus towered over him.

'Can you pay?' he demanded.

Ignus slapped a couple of coins onto the bar. The landlord eyed them sceptically.

'We'll be in the corner,' Ignus said. 'Bring us some food.'

The landlord swept the coins off the bar and bustled through a beaded doorway.

'Another happy Kerissian,' Quinn muttered.

They turned from the bar and made their way towards a table in the corner, well away from the other customers. Most of the men in the hostel had turned back to their drinks, but they were still drawing the occasional unfriendly glare.

'So, what's the plan?' Thea asked, while they waited for their food. She kept her voice down as low as possible.

'We stay the night here, then we carry on our quest,' Ignus started. 'We're going to need all of the Emperor's original Dragon Knights before we can hope to take on Vayn: Ulric, Nord, Kyria,

Taric and Noctaris, as well as me. Vayn's too powerful for just a couple of us, and he's had twelve years to perfect his sorcery.' He shook his head. 'Dark magic has twisted his mind. He won't care how many people he has to kill to stop us.'

'I'll use the sword,' Quinn said. 'That'll point us in the right direction.'

He glanced around to make sure he wasn't being watched. A hooded figure in the far corner was looking right at them. Quinn couldn't make out a face, but could see an elaborate brooch clasping the figure's cloak together and eyes boring into him like a drill.

Quickly, the figure looked away, suddenly concentrating hard on a mug of ale.

Quinn frowned, and shuffled closer to Thea. Once he was sure he was unobserved, he slowly drew out the tip of his father's golden sword. The sword had been used to knight the dragon-bloods in the first place – it had a connection to them. In the high tower back at Yaross Garrison, the sword had pointed in Ignus's direction. Somehow, it knew where to look for the dragons still bound by Vayn's magical copper manacles. But now, all Quinn could see in the blade was swirling mist and distant, indistinct shapes.

'That could be anywhere on Keriss Island,' Ignus grunted. 'The whole place is mostly one big swamp with a mountain in the middle and a couple of towns perched on the coast.'

'It's not much to go on to find the next Dragon Knight,' Quinn said, reluctantly.

'It'll still point us in the right direction,' Thea said hopefully. 'And it tells us he's definitely on this island.'

'Somewhere.'

The landlord appeared from behind the bar, carrying a plate of bread and cold meats. Quinn hushed as the man approached.

The landlord clattered the food down on the table in front of them. 'How long are you staying?' he demanded.

Ignus glanced at the food then around at the rest of the customers, who were still shooting ill-disposed glances in their direction. He met Quinn's eyes.

'Just one night. You can have too much of a good thing,' he laughed gruffly – though the landlord didn't seem to enjoy the joke. 'We'll travel inland to the main town tomorrow.'

Quinn noticed a moment of concern flash across the landlord's face.

'We're going to need supplies,' Ignus said. 'Food for the journey. Blankets. Some spare clothes.'

'I can sell you food,' the landlord barked, back to his grumpy self, 'but I can't help you with the rest.' With that, he turned away and hurried back to the bar.

'He really makes you feel welcome, doesn't he?' Thea laughed. 'Why do we need so many supplies?'

Ignus glanced around to make sure no one was listening, and then bent his head in close. 'We don't know where we're going to find the other Dragon Knights – they all went into exile when Vayn took the empire. We might need to search every one of the Twelve Islands . . . This is the start of a long journey.'

'We don't have *time* for a long journey,' Quinn

muttered. 'Vayn knows I'm alive and he knows you're free. He'll be looking for us.'

'Which is why we need to hurry,' Ignus said, 'and keep away from people as much as we can. Vayn will be circulating our descriptions to the Black Guard and their allies. People will be looking out for us.'

Thea let out a groan. 'Keep away from people? Look . . .'

The door to the hostel had opened and a new group were pushing their way inside. They were led by a man almost as big as Ignus. His face was covered in scars and lumps, as if he'd started his mornings by smashing his face against the nearest wall. His short hair was speckled with grey. Quinn saw the other customers look away, averting their eyes. When the landlord saw him, he hurried over, bowing like a worm.

'Bewick.' the landlord called, a shaky weasel grin spread across his face. He leant in close and whispered something. Bewick glanced over at Quinn with a scowl before he and his group crowded up at the bar and started drinking.

'I don't like the look of him,' Quinn said.

'I don't think he much likes the look of us, either,' Thea said. 'Keep your head down.'

Quinn, Thea and Ignus remained in their huddle, talking in low, hushed tones. However, Bewick's sharp voice rose from the direction of the bar, insistent.

'There are too many damned outsiders coming to this island,' he said loudly, wasting no time to demonstrate his malice.

Mutters of agreement rose around him.

'You know what I'd do?' Bewick continued. 'I'd sink their ships as soon as they got close to the shore. That'd keep them away.' He turned to glare across the room at Quinn, Thea and Ignus, then spat onto the dirty floor. Ignus ground his teeth, and Quinn saw the enormous muscles across his back tighten angrily.

'What *is* the problem with this place?' Ignus hissed under his breath.

Quinn reached out a hand to calm him, but could feel the heat coming off him in waves.

'Vermin, all of them,' Bewick called, casting

a sideways glance into the corner of the room.

Ignus slammed back his chair.

'Oh gods,' Thea muttered.

'What is your problem?' Ignus demanded, striding up to the group of men at the bar. His enormous hands were clenching into fists.

'My problem?' Bewick sneered. 'People have been disappearing – that's what my problem is. And you know who I blame? Outsiders like you. The last thing we need is more of you coming over here and making things worse.'

Quinn watched as Ignus's shoulders rolled threateningly.

'Me?' the Dragon Knight demanded. 'Make things worse? Worse than the Guard?'

Bewick pushed his stool aside, suddenly flaring. 'You're a damned outsider! Dare to disrespect the Guard and you can leave this island!'

He put his hands against Ignus's chest and shoved. The Dragon Knight took a step back and then swung his fist. It caught Bewick on the side of his face and sent him sprawling into his group of friends.

Bewick staggered to his feet again and launched himself back at Ignus, fists flying.

'I thought we were supposed to be keeping a low profile,' Quinn hissed, clutching his sword tight beneath the table.

'I don't think Ignus does low profile,' Thea said, her eyes darting about.

Great, Quinn thought. He wondered how long it would take for the landlord to call the Black Guard.

'Ignus!' Quinn shouted.

As the Dragon Knight turned to look back at Quinn and Thea, one of Bewick's blows rocketed against his ear. With a roar, Ignus grabbed Bewick and threw him bodily across the room, into a table. The table went flying, sending drinks scattering across the floor.

Suddenly the whole of the hostel erupted. Men were pushing and shoving each other, and punches started to fly. Bewick's friends threw themselves at Ignus, who scattered them with a great swing of his arm.

A flash of gold made Quinn look down. Bright

scales had appeared on his arm. He swore under his breath and pulled his sleeve down over them. *Why can't I control it? Why?* If someone spotted it, they would summon the Black Guard for sure.

'We need to get out of here,' Quinn said, grasping his satchel.

Thea met his eyes and nodded. 'Grab Ignus before he brings the whole town down on us.'

They darted across the hostel, dodging between struggling groups towards where Ignus was surrounded by half a dozen men. Quinn ducked a punch and skipped around a fallen table. Thea dashed along behind him. They had almost reached Ignus when a cluster of fighting men crashed right into them and Thea was sent skidding to the floor. One of the thugs grabbed hold of Quinn and shoved him back against the bar, trapping his arm behind him so he couldn't reach his sword. He could feel the man's sour breath as he leaned right over him. Quinn tried to struggle, straining against the man's weight, but slowly the man bent him over backwards.

'We don't . . . want . . . your . . . sort . . . around . . . here,' he said.

The man's arm across Quinn's throat was cutting off his breath. His vision was starting to go blurry at the edges. Gasping, he scrambled for something – anything – on the bar, but there was nothing in reach . . .

CHAPTER 3

A HELPING HAND

Quinn's head swirled and his ears roared as he fought for breath. Desperately, he swung his foot forwards as hard as he could.

He caught the man right between his legs. With a grunt, the man's hold on Quinn loosened and he dropped to the floor. Sucking in a breath, Quinn pushed free. He gasped and spluttered, rubbing at his sore throat.

Out of the corner of his eye he spotted Thea spring to her feet from where she'd fallen.

'Get back!' she cried, as black, roiling energy

sprang to life between her hands, and she began chanting under her breath.

Black smoke poured in great billows from her hands, suddenly filling the hostel.

'What is that?' the landlord shouted, panicked. Men raced for the door.

Quinn stumbled to his feet as Thea reached him.

'Where's Ignus?' Thea demanded. 'This will distract them – but not for long . . .'

A loud thump sounded from the smoke, and a man came stumbling back towards them. Quinn stepped out of the way.

'Over there would be my guess,' Quinn croaked, pointing to the figure of Bewick, who'd been hurled against the wall.

Together, they hurried into the smoke, where Ignus was parrying a blow. The smoke didn't seem to be affecting him – one of the benefits of being a fire dragon, Quinn supposed. Ignus was glaring around, looking for someone else to thump. His eyes lit up as Quinn and Thea emerged from the smoke, then his shoulders slumped.

'Oh,' he grunted. 'It's you.'

'Let's get out of here before someone calls the Guard,' Quinn said, coughing through the smoke. He grabbed Ignus by the arm, and he and Thea hauled the big man to the door.

They burst out into the street, eyes streaming. Quinn hurried them round the corner into a side alley, away from the drunken men in the tavern, and sucked in a great breath of clear air.

'Brilliant,' he said, angrily, glowering at Ignus. 'Now where are we going to go?' The first spots of cold rain were falling from the sky – Quinn peered around the edge of the building to see Bewick and his henchmen skulking off down the cobbled road. 'Are we supposed to sleep on the street?'

'He wasn't being very polite,' Ignus growled.

Quinn shook his head. This wasn't how it was supposed to be going. They were supposed to be tracking down the Dragon Knights one by one without anyone noticing them, until they were ready to face Vayn. If the Black Guard got wind of what had happened here, they'd be on to them. As though finding one of the Dragon Knights in the middle of the swamps wasn't hard enough.

'Look out,' Thea hissed.

A figure appeared at the end of the alley: the mysterious presence who'd been watching them at the hostel. Ignus grunted and clenched his fists again. Quinn let his hand drop to the hilt of his golden sword as he recognised the glittering brooch on the figure's cloak. Looking at it more clearly he could see it was an elegant bird, with jewelled eyes.

'It's all right,' a soft voice called.

A woman? Quinn thought.

The figure pulled back her hood to reveal long, oak-brown hair swept back from her high forehead and tucked behind her ears. She must have been around the same age as Ignus and she was nearly as tall – although not nearly as ugly.

'I saw you watching us earlier,' Quinn said. 'What do you want?'

She took another step closer. 'I can help you . . . if you let me.'

She didn't look particularly dangerous, but Quinn wasn't going to take a risk. She could be one of Vayn's spies.

'Maybe we don't need help.'

The woman laughed. 'You've just fled the only place in Port Keriss that's willing to accommodate strangers these days and this weather's going to get worse. I think you need my help.'

Quinn glanced at Ignus and Thea.

'Why should we trust you?' Thea asked.

The woman glanced around then moved closer to Quinn. 'Because I saw that flash of scales on your arm and didn't say a word. I could have gone to the Guard.'

Quinn's hand fell automatically to his sleeve. The scales were gone now, but he knew they could come back at any moment.

'And because I need your help.' Her head dropped. 'My name is Maria, and I need someone who will stand against the Black Guard . . .'

Quinn wavered.

'We haven't got anywhere else to go,' Thea whispered to him.

Quinn knew she was right. They couldn't stay out in the street all night. And Maria was telling the truth. She could have gone to the Guard. There was always a reward for turning in a dragonblood, and Quinn was pretty sure that reward would be far greater for turning in the true Emperor to Vayn.

'All right,' Quinn said. 'Let's talk.'

Quinn, Thea and Ignus made their way down the cobbled street. The howling of the wind and the rain lashing the rooftops was enough to convince them that they desperately needed shelter. Quinn had begun to dry out in the hostel, but now he was soaked through once more.

Maria led them to a small home above a strange-looking shop. Although shuttered for the night, Quinn caught a glimpse of jars of exotic spices through the grill.

The rooms had obviously been fairly grand once, but now the paint was peeling and the ceiling showed large damp stains from the rain. Maria lit a small fire in the grate and placed herself down delicately in a fraying armchair. Rain rattled against the cracked windowpanes.

'This is it,' she said, waving an arm to encompass the room. 'Make yourselves at home.'

Quinn lowered himself onto a sagging couch, which dipped even further beneath his weight. Ignus didn't even risk the furniture; he just hunched up against one wall. Quinn figured that was probably a good idea – the chairs didn't look like they could handle Ignus's muscly bulk.

'You know,' Maria began, 'you need to take care around Bewick.'

Ignus snorted. 'He's a weed.'

Maria shook her head. 'I can see you're a fighter. But Bewick is in league with Lorimer, and Lorimer is untouchable. He's one of Vayn's personal lord vassals. The Black Guard do whatever he says, and if you humiliate Bewick, Lorimer will take it personally.'

'Sounds like a great guy,' Ignus said. 'How does he get away with it?'

'He did something for Vayn a long time ago; a secret operation. It made him one of Vayn's favourites. He's lived in Astria like a king ever since. He's got a whole suite in the old castle the Black Guard are using as their fort.'

'Astria?' Quinn asked, frowning.

'The main town on the Island. It's in the valley on the other side of the marshes. That's how I used to make my living, trading stuff that came in to the port to Astria. I did pretty well out of it.' She sighed and looked around at the decrepit room. 'Now this is all I've got left; this and the shop downstairs.'

'So what happened?' Thea asked. 'Why can't you trade?'

'I do.' She dropped her voice, 'But when Vayn took over, the Black Guard seized the main road across the island. That's when things got bad. If you use the road, you have to pay their taxes, which means they take at least half of everything you have. But this last year, it's got much worse. Now if anyone tries to use the road, the Guard steal everything you've got.'

Another gift from Vayn, Quinn thought. He had never known his father, Marek, but he did know the Twelve Islands hadn't been like that when he'd been Emperor. Quinn felt the now familiar dragonblood course through his veins.

'The only other way to get to Astria is via the paths through the marshes,' Maria continued, 'and they're always shifting. People go missing when they use that route.'

So Bewick was right, Quinn thought. *No wonder we've had such a frosty reception.*

'But that's not all . . . ' Maria gathered her cloak about her, shivering. She looked pained as she began to speak. 'If the marshes don't swallow you up, the Stone Trolls might.'

'The what?' Quinn began.

Ignus guffawed. 'Kerissian Stone Trolls? They're stuff and nonsense! A myth!'

Maria snapped back, 'They *were* myths,' she scowled. 'But not any more. Vayn brought them into existence.

Ignus looked taken aback as Maria continued.

'Keriss kept fighting against him even after the

Emperor and Empress were gone, so he used his dark magic to turn rock into the horrific creatures of myth and legend. They're shaped like men, but twice your size' – she nodded at Ignus – 'and made completely of stone. You can't hurt them and you can't reason with them. They're only loyal to Vayn. They stalk the marshes and they'll attack anyone or anything they come across, ordinary people or Black Guard. It's almost impossible to trade safely any more.' She looked around her room. 'You might not guess it, but a lot of people are doing even worse than me now. What's the good of a port if you can't trade anything?'

'You said you needed our help,' Quinn reminded her.

'Lorimer and Bewick are too powerful. I can't trust anyone in Port Keriss, but you're strangers, and you're not exactly Bewick's best friends right now. It's my cousin, Anna. She disappeared. She was crossing the marshes to Astria, and she was supposed to be back a week ago. I'm terrified that something's happened to her. If you can help me, I can guide you through the marshes in return.' She glanced at the windows again. Dark clouds were racing across the sky, obscuring the moon and the stars, and rain spattered down, hitting the windows with the force of a hail-storm. 'I have nothing against dragonbloods. I remember the Empire before Vayn and his Black Guard, and I've heard a rumour. They say the true Emperor has returned.' She met Quinn's eyes. 'He'd be about your age now.'

Quinn pulled his hair out of his face and looked up at the others. 'What do you think?'

'If the Stone Trolls are real, we can't just go stomping across the marsh,' Ignus said. 'I've seen them. We'd be lost in there on our own.'

'Then it's agreed,' Thea said. 'We'll set off in the morning.' She turned to glare at Ignus. 'And this time, let's try and keep a low profile . . . No more picking fights.'

Quinn nodded. They had to keep unnoticed and away from the Black Guard. Though something told him that would be easier said than done.

CHAPTER 4

SHADOWS IN THE MIST

They left Port Keriss at first light.

Maria hadn't had much in her home, but she'd managed to find a few spare clothes and backpacks for each of them, and some provisions. She'd even helped Quinn mend his shoes, which had begun to fall to pieces from being soaked repeatedly in seawater. For the first time in days, Quinn had had a decent breakfast and he was feeling confident about the journey ahead. He'd also managed to pull a brush through his tangled hair and give his face a scrub.

The rain had died out during the night and

in its place mist had slipped in from the marshes, covering the small port like a cold, wet cloth. The air was sharp and the wind chilly, as they moved down the narrow streets to the inland town gate – where they left the suspicious locals – and out onto the main highway that led to Astria. Every footstep and clink of metal from their gear seemed dulled by the mist.

The ragtag group hadn't gone more than half a mile from the port when the road began to dip down from the rocky coastline and away from the stormy sea. The cold became more and more intense until Quinn could feel goosebumps break out across his body.

'This is as far as we go on the road,' Maria huffed, as the land levelled out and the marshes stretched out around them. Quinn saw tall, skeletal trees looming out of the stagnant water, draped with hanging mosses that dripped slowly into the marsh.

Maria pointed an elegant hand across the marsh. 'Follow me exactly,' she said. 'The paths can shift in an instant. One false move and the ground will swallow you whole.'

With a long, last look at the solid, straight highway cutting through middle of the marshes, Quinn stepped off the road behind Maria. Thea shot a protective, sideways glance his way.

From the road, it had seemed like there were dozens of paths and ways between the pools of still, dirty water. However, up close, Quinn could see that some of what had looked like solid land was no more than clumps of grass floating above the surface. The ground where they stepped was boggy and wet, and water bubbled up over his shoes until his feet were soaked again. He heard Ignus curse behind him as the big man sank to his knees.

'*Exactly* where I tread,' Maria called back.

Slowly they trudged through the marshes, sometimes doubling back, sometimes circling around. Quinn couldn't see the sun through the mist and he had no idea in what direction they were actually heading. For all he knew, Maria could be leading them right to a patrol of Black

Guard. *But why would she do that?* he thought. If she'd wanted to turn them in, she could have done it in the middle of the port and saved herself a grim trudge in the cold.

It was the mist that was making him feel paranoid. Its presence felt a little too real, pressing in from all sides, drifting up through his cotton shawl and tunic. It was as if the ghosts of the marsh's victims were reaching up one more time . . .

'You're going crazy,' he muttered to himself.

Ignus must have heard him, and soon broke the silence. 'Who's for a marching song?'

'Aren't you worried about being heard?' Thea said.

'No one's going to hear us out here,' Maria said.

'Oh,' Thea said. 'Good. I don't suppose you're actually any good at singing?' she asked Ignus.

As it turned out, he wasn't, but at least his bellowing, out-of-tune voice seemed to make the mist and marshes feel less eerie. Quinn couldn't imagine any kind of ghost world where there would be such a loud and tuneless song. With

Ignus beside him, what could he have to worry about? The man was a *flame dragon* after all, and even when he wasn't in his dragonform, he could flatten most opponents with one of his meaty fists.

As the marsh path widened, Thea, sure-footed and nimble, skipped easily alongside Maria and soon fell into conversation about the exotic-looking ingredients on display in her shop – *magic* ingredients, for potion making. Quinn, however, dropped back until he was walking alongside Ignus. The further they moved into the marshes, the thicker the mist became. By now, Quinn could scarcely see his hand in front of his face.

As Ignus took a breath between his tuneless verses, Quinn let his thoughts burst out. 'Dragonform,' he practically shouted. 'What's the deal?'

'I was wondering when you were going to ask that,' Ignus rumbled. He took a deep breath, and put a huge, protective arm around Quinn's shoulder. 'They say it's to do with emotion: anger, hatred, love – mixed with dragonblood, of course – passed down from the ancients, when magic and dragons were more common on these isles than they are now.'

'And the powers?' Quinn asked. 'You're "flame", others are "storm" and "shadow" . . .'

'That all depends,' Ignus said. 'All dragons can breathe fire – but you won't find a flame stronger than a flame dragon's. I always expected to be a dragon; it wasn't a secret back then and it nearly always ran in my family. But it still came as a surprise to me.'

'What happened?' Quinn asked.

'Well, I was fighting with my brother. One minute we were wrestling on the ground, the next, I felt scales springing up on my skin, and my bones stretching and bending . . .'

Quinn knew that feeling . . . being under threat, the hot dragonblood coursing through his body.

'Then,' Ignus continued, 'wings burst through my back, and I was looking at the world through the eyes of a dragon and I knocked my brother halfway across the field. You should have seen the look on his face!'

'And now . . .?'

'Now it just happens. I get the image of the dragon in my mind and I think about how it feels to change. It's as natural as breathing.'

Quinn wanted to kick Ignus in his giant shin. *It just happens?* Not to Quinn, it didn't. Ignus was obviously a natural, whereas Quinn felt like a fraud. *And I'm the one who's supposed to be the true Emperor?*

He ground his teeth and focused all his concentration, remembering the moment he had lashed out at Goric, the Black Guard captain on Yaross – although he wouldn't make much of an Emperor if that was all he could manage. Back then, talons had sprung out from his fingers without him even thinking about it, and scales had covered his arm to deflect Goric's magic sword. He pulled the images up into his mind, forced himself to remember the heat racing across his skin, and the tingling, twisting of his flesh. *Become scales, please.*

A patch of golden scales appeared on his hand for a moment, itching like he'd reached into a patch of stinging nettles, then faded again. He kicked a tussock of boggy grass in frustration.

Suddenly, a scream sounded up ahead. Quinn jumped, snatched out of his concentration and back to reality.

Thea?

'What was that?' Ignus barked.

Quinn put his head down and broke into a run, splashing through the cold, muddy water. He found his hand had drawn his sword without him even thinking about it. Ignus leapt after him, charging like a bull.

Together, Quinn and Ignus burst out onto a little hillock that rose above the mist. Thea had dropped to her knees on the wet grass and was almost doubled over laughing. Maria was looking down at her slightly disapprovingly.

'What is it?' Ignus demanded, steam drifting from his nose and mouth to thicken the already heavy mist.

'Sorry,' Thea said, trying to muffle her laughs. She waved a hand towards a twisted tree stump sticking out of the bog. Mist wreathed around it, stirring gently in an unseen breeze. 'I just got "attacked" by a Kerissian Stone Troll.' She took a steadying breath.

Quinn gave a laugh and pulled Thea to her feet. 'I think this mist might be getting to you.'

'Maybe we should travel closer together,' Ignus said, seriously. 'If one of us *really* gets in trouble, we can't afford to be separated.'

'OK,' said Quinn. But instead of keeping close, he let the others stride ahead. He'd almost had it, his dragonform; he wasn't about to give up now.

As they continued to make their way carefully through the marshes, the chill deepening all the while, Quinn still held back. Leeches crawled across the ground and over his boots. He peeled them off and threw them back in the marsh water.

He pushed his hair back from his eyes and gathered his thoughts once more. He wasn't going to give up on his father's inheritance so easily. *I'm going to figure it out if it takes me the rest of my life.*

He could still hear the voices of the others up ahead. As long as he could hear them, he figured he'd be fine.

Concentrate!

He pictured the dragonform he'd seen reflected in his golden sword. That was how he'd known he was a dragonblood in the first place. In the sword, he'd been covered in fine, glistening golden scales. He tried imagining his arms coated with those steel-hard bright scales. He let his mind melt into the image until he could feel the heat almost burning at the underside of his skin, which was itching so badly he wanted to tear it off.

Change!

His skin started to harden in front of his eyes, the lightly tanned colour deepening and becoming golden until the skin had become overlapping scales. Slowly, they crept up his arm, all the way to his shoulder. *Yes!* This was the most he'd ever managed, and the scales weren't fading. *Now, my legs.* He pictured them in his mind like the legs of the dragon in the sword. Fire raced along his veins, flaring and burning. He reached down to feel his legs under the cotton trousers, and felt the scales appear at his thighs and work their way down.

Suddenly, as the scales reached his knees he realised his mistake. His legs gave way completely and he stumbled forward, the support gone from under him.

'Argh . . .' He let out a quick cry before tumbling into the black water with a splash. The weight of his clothes and his backpack dragged him down, the murky water closed over his head and he soon disappeared under the misty surface. No matter how hard he kicked his useless legs, he kept on sinking.

The dragonform was dragging him down and the weight of the golden scales was keeping him under. He tried to let out a scream but instead just gulped down the nasty black water; bubbles coursed from his mouth, rising upwards like a final prayer.

Quinn turned his head desperately. The water was dark and full of cloying mud and weeds. His clothes felt like they were made out of metal.

There! his mind screamed. Above him was the faint light of the surface. It seemed so far away.

Let go of it! Think of something else. Anything! He forced the image of the scales out of his mind and suddenly he felt his flesh return.

He kicked and pulled with his arms, forcing himself upwards, dragging himself through the tangle of weeds that threatened to lure him towards a watery grave. His lungs burned, demanding air. *Just keep going!*

Finally, his head burst from the surface. He coughed violently, dredging up the black water he'd swallowed, gasping for the misty air surrounding him.

'Urgh-gh,' he gurgled, fighting the urge to vomit as more brackish water rose in his throat. He flailed for a grassy mound and caught hold of it. With the last of his strength, he managed to haul himself halfway out, his feet still dangling in the marshy wetness. His body shuddered as he drew in great, rasping breaths. He cursed himself for losing sight of the marsh path and his fellow travellers.

Then something emerged from the mist. 'Ignus!' he called, relieved.

But he soon realised it wasn't the fire dragon. Instead, the figure was vast and horned. As it loomed over him and reached out he saw that whatever it was, it clearly wasn't human.

'Not I, my friend,' it began. 'Guess again . . .'

5

AND THEN, HE WAS GONE

Quinn grasped at the marsh reeds, his heart thumping with fear.

The creature above him looked like a man, but it was far bigger. Gigantic horns jutted from its forehead and a black mask covered its face. Its fingers ended in jagged yellow claws. *A Stone Troll?* Quinn wondered.

With a yell, Quinn thrashed his feet and hauled himself upwards, but the giant horned creature was too quick. It lunged and grabbed Quinn around the throat. He felt its claws digging into his neck as it dragged him out of the marsh water.

Not a Stone Troll. . . he thought. *Definitely something worse. . .*

'I've got a choice for you, my friend,' the creature growled. 'It's an easy one: your money, or your life.'

Quinn closed his eyes and tried to concentrate. He'd been so close to getting his dragonform until he'd fallen into the marsh. If it would just come to him now . . .

The giant shook him. 'Well?'

Quinn couldn't focus. Not with those claws against his throat. He'd have to use brute force . . .

'How . . . about . . .' he gasped. '*Your* life!'

Quinn kicked out and felt his foot drive home into the giant's soft belly. With a whoosh of breath the giant dropped him, cursing. The moment he hit the ground, Quinn dragged his sword from his scabbard and swung it with all his force at the giant.

'Raarghh,' he yelled, charging.

The giant jumped back, dodging Quinn's blow. Suddenly, his fearsome bluster was gone, and a look of panic swept across his ugly face.

'Now hold on, hold on!' He held up his hands. 'You don't want to do this. No reason we can't do it nicely. Just hand over your money and no one needs to get hurt.'

'Oh yeah?' Quinn laughed, mockingly. 'How about when you had me by the neck?'

He took a step forward, raising his sword; the giant stumbled in the boggy ground.

'You're taking this far too personally,' he said, not half as fierce-sounding as he had been a moment ago. In fact, Quinn reckoned he was looking a bit pale around the mask now. Maybe he wasn't used to people fighting back.

'You think this is too personal?' Quinn growled. 'You haven't seen anything yet.'

With a yell, he charged the giant, swinging his sword in a great arc over his head. The giant stumbled back, raising his arms. Then, something strange happened. As Quinn brought down the golden sword, it sliced right through his attacker as though he wasn't there. The giant tumbled back, hitting the wet ground with a dull splash.

The giant's form seemed to shift and shudder, cast off like the mist evaporating in the sun's glare. Quinn was no longer looking at the terrifying horned monster from just a moment ago. Instead, in front of him lay a thin, scruffy-looking man with a scraggly moustache, holding up his arms in defence.

Quinn lowered his sword. 'What the . . .?' he managed.

'Ah,' the man said, clearing his throat. 'About that . . .'

At that moment, the mist parted and Ignus, Thea and Maria came charging out.

'What's happening?' Thea demanded. 'What's going on?'

Quinn pointed at the man on the ground. 'I don't know, but this man has some explaining to do . . .'

Maria looked down at the puny figure. 'And

I thought you might have found a Stone Troll
. . .'

Ignus charged forward, his fists at the ready.
However, as he stepped closer, dodging the peat
bogs and grimy water, a smirk began to creep
across his face. As he loomed over the 'giant',
he let out a great guffaw of laughter.

'What's so funny?' Quinn demanded.

Ignus just ignored him and held out a hand
into the bog. 'Ulric, you old fraud!' he bellowed.
'What in Alariss are you doing with your back-
side in a peat bog?'

'Ulric?' Quinn demanded.

'The Dragon Knight?' Thea gawped.

'That's me,' the man said, sheepishly. 'The
Shadow Dragon.' Ulric sketched a little bow as
Ignus hauled the soaking wet man to his feet.

'Where in the gods' blue sky have you been,
old friend?' Ignus boomed, grabbing Ulric in a
friendly bear hug.

'Uh, well,' Ulric stammered, freeing himself
from Ignus's breath-crushing embrace. 'That's a
long story . . .'

'I'll help fill you in,' Quinn began, angrily. 'This man was trying to rob me!'

Ignus let out another roar of laughter, clutching at his stomach.

Thea stared at the big man. 'Why is this so funny?'

'It's not!' Quinn fumed.

Ignus grinned at Ulric. 'It's good to see you, old man. I thought you were going to hide out on Duna, or Aya Nor?'

'Too cold for my tastes.' Ulric laughed, but then turned serious. 'Although it's not exactly paradise here on Keriss. Things have been bad, Ignus. Since I've had this manacle round my ankle, it's been tough to get by. The Black Guard has things controlled pretty tightly, particularly in Astria. I've had to survive any way I could.'

'By robbing people?' Quinn demanded. 'That's what the Dragon Knights have been reduced to? Common thieves?'

Ulric straightened and patted down his clothes. 'Not *common* thieves. A very *uncommon* one, actually. Anyway, it's not like I keep all the money for myself, and I only rob the rich. I give the money to locals. There's no way they can make a living with the Black Guard and the Stone Trolls making trade almost impossible. And I never actually *hurt* anyone, I just scare them.'

'So it *is* true,' Maria gasped. 'I've heard of the Horned Highwayman. Not everyone is best pleased . . .'

'Well, the *rich* wouldn't be,' Ulric laughed cheerily. With his face creasing, it looked like his moustache had a life of its own.

'It's not just that,' Maria continued, seriously. 'I've heard people blame you for the disappearances in the marshes.'

Ulric looked grave, but dismissed the suggestion airily. 'But everyone knows that's those hideous Stone Trolls, surely?'

'That doesn't matter to the Guard. They'll blame anyone rather than do something about the trolls.'

Quinn frowned. There was one thing that had been bugging him. 'I thought you lost your dragon powers when you were bound. How were you able to change shape like that?'

'Ah,' Ulric sighed. 'I lost my dragon powers when Vayn put these manacles on my ankle, yes, but I still have a small remnant of my shadow abilities in my human form. Although, what you saw was just a weak echo. You should have seen me before I was bound.'

'That's right,' Ignus continued. 'As a human I, too, can use my flame powers in a small way, to light fires and such. But it's when I'm in my dragonform that I can really harness my abilities.'

'I get it,' Thea said. 'You have an ability, but your dragonform enhances it.'

'That's it,' Ignus replied. 'So, shadow dragons like Ulric can project images into people's minds. Like the fear of what lurks in dark corners at night, they can make themselves appear as something completely different to what they are – at least until someone like Quinn breaks the illusion with a sword. Once, when the old Emperor Marek had only just united the islands, Ulric appeared as Lord Vayn in a jester's outfit for a whole week.'

'And I'm not sure he ever forgave me,' Ulric said, with a dark smile.

Ignus guffawed and clapped Ulric on the shoulder, almost knocking the scrawny man into the pool of black water. 'Ulric, my friend, things are going to change. You have had the enormous good fortune of attempting to rob the son of the Emperor Marek himself. This is Quinn, the lost Emperor of the Twelve Islands of Alariss, and the boy who's going to send Vayn back down to the demonic plains. Isn't that right, Quinn?'

Ulric squinted suspiciously. 'Are you trying to trick me again, Ignus? You know you can't trick a shadow dragon.'

'He's telling the truth,' Thea said.

'Look!' Ignus said, rolling up his trousers. Where his manacles had once bound him, there were nothing but faint scars around his ankles. 'He knighted me again and freed me from Vayn's bonds. He is the true Emperor. He's going to free us all and we'll take back our kingdom. You're going to be free again, my man.'

Quinn glared at the scrawny Dragon Knight who had tried to rob him only minutes earlier.

'Yeah,' he said, gruffly. 'I wouldn't be too sure about that if I were you . . .'

CHAPTER 6

THE STONE WOMAN

Ignus flashed a hard stare in Quinn's direction, his black eyes like burning coals.

'What are you talking about?' he demanded. 'Free him. He's one of your knights.'

'Yeah, Quinn,' Thea said. 'We need him.'

'He tried to rob me!' Quinn shook his head angrily. 'He didn't know who I was, but that didn't stop him. How am I supposed to trust him?'

It didn't help that he was soaked to the bone and covered in freezing marsh water. It didn't help that he couldn't control his dragonform when he needed to most. It didn't help that someone like

Ulric could potentially turn into a dragon when he couldn't. And for all Quinn knew, Ulric had been stealing from people for a long time. That made him as bad as the Black Guard.

The others looked at him in frustration.

'I'm *sorry*,' Ulric said, with a flourish. 'But you don't know what it's been like on Keriss. The people have suffered.'

Quinn looked Ulric up and down with suspicion. On the one hand he was a Dragon Knight, one of his sworn protectors, but right now, he looked like nothing but a common thief, his once red, dirty rags dragging on the ground behind him. As the others looked on, Quinn made his decision.

'You can join us,' he said stiffly, shoving his sword back in his scabbard and stalking away across the marshes. 'But you'll have to prove you're worthy. Only then will I free you . . .'

As darkness fell across the marshes, they faced spending the night under the stars. Maria scoured the landscape for a safe, dry place to camp, eventually finding a grassy mound that jutted a few feet above the marsh. Ulric tagged along with them, caught between the desire to be free and the shame of being shunned by Quinn. He wore a weary expression, trying to remain proud and cheery, but underneath it all, frustrated. The five of them huddled together in the shelter of a few stunted trees that clung to life in the middle of the barren bogs.

'I used to camp here with my cousin,' Maria said sadly, as she huddled down, peering into the mist that surrounded them.

'We'll find her,' Thea said, sounding more confident than she looked.

Ignus built a fire with branches from the dead trees, igniting it with his breath – Quinn used the heat to dry his sodden clothes.

Beyond the light of the campfire, all was darkness. The marshes were even more eerie than in the day. Creatures shrieked and called across the water and unknown things splashed heavily into pools just yards away from them. Quinn barely slept, thinking long into the night about Ulric and wondering if he'd done the right thing. His thoughts fell back to his Aunt Marta – she always had good judgement – and the parents he never knew: Marek, his father, and Isaria, his mother. What would they have done? What had happened to them, really? What was the Empire like when they ruled?

When the grey light of dawn finally climbed over the horizon, the mist rolled across the land, as thick and cold ever. It seemed like it never moved; maybe it would bathe the land in its ghostly light forever. After a quick breakfast of dry biscuits and a thin porridge Maria had supplied, they set off across the marshes once more.

'This part of the swamp doesn't change much,' Maria said. 'The ground's firmer. We're through the worst of it.'

Quinn strode out ahead, not wanting to be near Ulric. He felt embarrassed by how easily he'd been taken in by a mirage. He was supposed to be a dragonblood and an emperor! He'd been as scared as a little boy.

But I sent you flying in the end, he thought.

'I think you're being too hard on him,' Thea
called. Quinn looked around to see that Thea had
come to walk alongside him. He'd been so
wrapped up in his thoughts he hadn't even noticed.

'No I'm not!' Quinn snapped. 'He's a thief,
isn't he? I have to be able to trust the Dragon
Knights. If you want to trust him, that's up to
you, but you're not the Emperor and you don't
have to take responsibility.'

'You're not the Emperor, either!' Thea cried.
'Not yet anyway.'

Quinn felt his cheeks burning as he realised
how arrogant he'd sounded.

'Maybe you should stop acting like you're the
only one who matters here. We're all in this
together, and we're doing it for you!'

'Sorry,' Quinn mumbled. He cleared his throat
awkwardly. He hadn't meant to take it out on
Thea. Ever since the garrison back on Yaross
she'd been by his side. She hadn't known her
parents either and she was just as determined
to stop the Black Guard.

'You're right,' he said, brushing back the hair

that had fallen into his face. 'But we have to be sure.'

'I hope he proves "worthy" soon,' she said. 'We'll need all the help we can get.'

Quinn charged on, changing the subject. 'I've been thinking about that – maybe my Aunt Marta would know what to do.' His aunt had been one of Empress Isaria's ladies-in-waiting. She'd raised Quinn as her own child, and when the Black Guard had taken Quinn she'd tried to help him escape.

'I never even got a chance to find out what happened to her. And I never got a chance to ask her about my parents. I know their ship went down' – he shuddered, thinking of those heaving, rocky seas around Keriss Island.

'I've been thinking the same thing,' Thea said, softening. 'Whatever it was, it could have something to do with Bewick and the Lord of Keriss. We'll find a way to contact Aunt Marta.'

Quinn nodded, but he wasn't sure if Thea was just saying it. After all, what was she going to do? Even if Marta wasn't in a dungeon somewhere, she could be anywhere on the Twelve Islands.

Suddenly, there was a call behind them.

Quinn whirled around, his hand dropping again to his sword, but he couldn't see anything in the thick mist. Thea peered about, her hands held ready, as though she was about to cast a spell.

'Come on!' Quinn said, dashing away into the mist. They'd become separated from Ignus, Maria and Ulric.

Quinn leapt over a small puddle, his feet splashing the edge of the stagnant water, then sprinted across the sodden grass. With every step, the ground threatened to give way and send him tumbling into the marsh again. He wasn't even sure he was running in the right direction because of the thickness of the mist.

He burst out of the fog in time to see Ignus, Ulric and Maria staring at something half submerged in the water. It looked human, but it wasn't moving, and as far as Quinn could see, it was made of stone.

Quinn's heart jumped as he saw it. 'A troll?' he demanded, as Thea came up beside him.

Maria shook her head. 'No. They're bigger. *Much* bigger . . .'

Quinn frowned. It looked like a statue, desperately trying to haul itself out of the mire.

'. . . and that,' she continued, 'is what happens when a Stone Troll catches you.'

Quinn peered closer. The figure's eyes were wide and his mouth was open as though he'd been screaming for his life. Quinn reached a hand forward. Instead of colourful robes there was dull, lifeless grey. Instead of warm skin, there was only rough stone beneath his fingertips. Hair, clothes, skin, everything, had been turned to dull, solid stone. As he pulled his fingers away, a small fragment of rock from the man's cloak crumbled away.

'Agh!' he cried.

'Get back!' Maria called . . . 'You'll *break* him.'

Quinn flinched away, leaving the poor man trapped. He wondered if there was still part of him that knew what was happening . . .

'We must tread carefully, friends,' Ulric whispered solemnly. 'The trolls could be close.'

Cautiously, the group crept through the marshes, peering into the freezing mist at every dark shape that loomed out at them. Here and there, they saw other petrified people, turned to stone by the touch of the Stone Trolls. No wonder no one wanted to cross the marshes. Get robbed on the road by the Black Guard – or Ulric – or take your chances with the Stone Trolls. Quinn clenched his fists. *This is Vayn's fault. All of it.*

The path they were on turned sharply to the left, leading between a couple of thick, stunted trees, before emerging on the edge of a wide pond. Around it more stone figures loomed out of the mist: what looked like a travelling party, ambushed . . .

Maria rushed across to the group and screamed as her worst fears were confirmed. 'No,' she gasped, as she passed between the trees and came out by the pool. She dropped to her knees.

'What is it?' Ignus said, crossing over to her.

Maria pointed with one shaking hand. Near

the edge of the pool was another stone figure, this time of a young woman. Quinn didn't recognise the woman, but he knew instinctively who it was.

'My cousin,' Maria sobbed. 'That's *Anna*.'

CHAPTER 7

SHADOW AT THE GATE

Quinn gawped in horror at the figure in the water. Anna must have leapt from the path to escape the Stone Troll. She was reaching out with one arm, as though to swim away out of reach, but she'd been too late. It must have grabbed her and instantly turned her to stone.

Maria bent over her, weeping. 'This is my fault,' she whispered between wracking sobs. 'I sent her to Astria. We needed to deliver our cargo. We'd done the trip together before, but I had to . . . I had to wait for a new delivery.' She reached out a hand towards her cousin.

'Here,' Ignus said. 'Let me lift her out of there. Ulric, help me.'

Together, Ignus and Ulric gently heaved the stone body out of the marsh and laid it on the path. Maria bent over her cousin, her hand brushing Anna's lifeless stone cheeks.

'We'll destroy the Stone Trolls,' Thea said, fiercely. 'We'll find a way to help your cousin and all the others. Magic made the trolls and magic can stop them. Somehow.'

'I promise you,' Quinn said. His voice didn't sound quite like his own. It sounded deeper and older. Maybe it was because his throat felt so tight. Maria looked up at him gratefully.

'We should get out of the marshes,' Ulric said, glancing around. 'We won't be able to help anyone if we're turned into statues ourselves. Come on! It's not far to Astria.'

'I can't leave her,' Maria protested, still staring down at her petrified cousin. 'Not like this.'

'We can't take her. You saw what happened to the other stone figure . . . You said it yourself.

If we take her with us she risks –' But Ignus didn't finish his sentence; the look on Maria's face stopped him. Quinn knew what he was about to say. *She risks crumbling to pieces.*

Reluctantly, Maria got to her feet and looked into her cousin's eyes. 'All right. But we *will* come back here.'

'We will,' Quinn said. 'No matter what.'

With a last long look back at her cousin, Maria led the way quietly through the marshes, but the sombre mood permeated the entire group.

Ulric was right; Astria wasn't far ahead. After another hour or so of walking through the marshes, the path began to rise and the boggy ground fell behind. The mist finally thinned then cleared, and up ahead, Quinn saw the walls of the town rise above him.

Set on a plain leading back down to the sea on one side and up into the rocky, uneven hills on the other, Astria balanced in the middle like a lazy cat. A fortified wall stretched across the whole front of the valley, cutting the town off from the marshes and, Quinn reckoned, from anyone who might want to attack it.

It also meant that there was no way in except via the enormous wooden gates that stood at the end of the main road. The gates were studded with iron to strengthen them against assault, and the black fist of Emperor Vayn had been crudely hammered onto the wood. Quinn could still see where the symbol of the blazing sun of his father had been ripped away, leaving a fading scar. Vayn's flags fluttered over the gatehouse.

There were half a dozen sentries at the gate, staring out over the marsh.

'Great,' Maria whispered. 'Just what we need.'

'How are we going to get past?' Quinn whispered.

'Just follow my lead,' Maria said. 'And do as I say.'

The group pulled their shawls about them and tried to look as inconspicuous as possible – that wasn't exactly easy because they were the only people approaching.

As they came nearer the guards drew to attention. Their burly leader, too fat for the armour that was desperately trying to contain his gut, called a halt on the group. 'Stop right there,' he cried. 'State your business!'

Maria stepped forward. 'We've come from Port Keriss. I'm a trader in fine spices. I've brought samples.' She pulled out a pouch and opened it, showing several small packets.

The fat guard grumbled and leaned over to inspect them. His eyes watered as he sniffed up the powerful mixtures. Quinn tried not to snigger as the guard let out a giant sneeze.

'Pfft!' he spluttered. 'Gods! Who wants that muck? Do you think anyone in Astria will pay for those?'

A second guardsman shouldered forward, pushing Maria out of the way. He towered over the others. Quinn prayed to the gods Ignus would contain his rage, as the tall, spindly guardsman looked them up and down.

Maria wouldn't be intimidated. 'Lord Lorimer seems to like them,' she huffed.

Quinn had no idea if Lord Lorimer was a fan of pungent spices or not, but at the mention of his name, the guard's attitude soon changed. He suddenly turned to attention, tucking another fold of flab into his armour and looking nervously round to his fellow guards.

'V-very well,' he snorted. 'I suppose if it's for Lorimer, then—'

'Wait!' the second guard cried.

Uh oh. Quinn's mind went into overdrive.

The lanky guard moved through the crowd until he stopped directly in front of Quinn. He glared down and peered into his amber eyes. Quinn tried to dodge his gaze, but there was no escaping it.

'What have we got here?' hissed the guard. 'I think I recognise this one . . .'

Vayn, Quinn thought. He must be on to them. Maybe there were posters round the island: *WANTED* posters. His image was probably at every checkpoint in the Twelve Islands by now – he was stupid to think he could defeat the Guard on Yaross and for there not to be any consequences.

'I-I doubt it,' he said, thinking on his feet. He tried to sound as meek as possible, keeping his eyes trained on the ground. 'I'm from the northern islands, it's my first time on Keriss . . .'

The guard smirked, not believing him for a moment. Quinn could feel Ignus and Thea bristle by his side . . .

'You're that boy, from Yaross.' He called to his fellow guards. 'Let me get a closer look at you, you worm,' He reached out to grab Quinn, who tried to get away but the guard was on him too fast. *This is it,* Quinn thought, *we'll have to fight* . . . The guard reached for Quinn's hood and pulled it back with a gleeful flourish . . . Quinn felt something grab his wrist.

'A-ha,' cried the guard, but then a look of confusion crossed his face. 'What the—'

Quinn sucked in a breath and looked around at the astonished faces of Ignus and Thea. He could feel the breeze rustling gently across his face, but something was different. He went to run a hand through his shoulder-length hair, but instead felt only bristly stubble. He looked down at his hand, which was suddenly bone white and covered in tiny blond hairs, instead of the normal tanned, smooth skin. As he exhaled his panicked breath, it felt different. He reached up to rub what turned out to be a crooked nose.

'You fool!' bellowed the fat guard to the lanky guard. 'He's an old man! Let them pass, before we have Lord Lorimer to contend with for holding up his shipment . . .'

'We're free to go?' Maria asked hopefully.

The guardsman in front of Quinn blinked in confusion like a gormless fish. 'I . . .' he muttered. 'Um . . .'

Quinn looked down at the hand clamped round his wrist: Ulric. He gave Quinn a sly grin and a wink. His eyes flashed at the bemused-looking guard. Not wasting any time, the others barrelled through the checkpoint. Quinn pulled up his hood and hurried behind them, Ulric dragging him along impatiently.

Ignus and Thea hurried around them, as they made their way swiftly away from the checkpoint and down the mud path towards the first shops and houses in the town.

'What *is* that?' Thea asked breathlessly. 'Magic? Is it a spell . . .?'

'Quinn, you look like an ancient old bruiser,' Ignus laughed. 'Like me!'

Ulric let go of his tight grip on Quinn's hand and suddenly the mirage dropped. Quinn's features softened and turned back to normal. His nose straightened out, his arms darkened, and he had the strange sensation of feeling his hair grow back down to his shoulders all at once.

He looked up at Ulric. 'I have no idea . . .'

Ulric gave a cheeky grin, his moustache dancing on his upper lip. 'That, my friends, is a little taste of Shadow Magic!' he declared. 'And I don't like to brag . . .'

Quinn doubted that very much – he could feel the pride coming off Ulric in waves.

'. . . But it's just a little trick I learnt long ago,' he continued. 'If I hold on to someone else, I can project my abilities onto them, too.'

'That's amazing,' Thea gasped.

'Not bad, eh, Quinn?' Ignus boomed.

Quinn couldn't deny the relief that was coursing through him. Despite Ulric's arrogance, Quinn could recognise a good deed when he saw one.

'Yeah, pretty amazing,' he muttered to Ulric. 'I guess you saved us.'

CHAPTER 8

A CRY FOR HELP

The first thing Quinn noticed as they walked through Astria was how desperate it looked. The roofs of the old houses which lined the streets had missing tiles and the windows had wooden hoardings instead of glass. Pale pink paintwork was peeling, and in places, whole walls had crumbled.

Maria shook her head as they made their way down towards the market. 'It wasn't this bad last time I was here. It gets worse every visit,' she muttered.

People scurrying through the damp, cobbled

streets threw them suspicious glances before hurrying away once more. The five of them continued through the winding streets until they eventually opened out onto a large square. The ground was paved with faded marble making intricate, beautiful art. The lamps that hung in straight lines around the perimeter were wrought in curving, unusual designs. The whole place looked like it had once been prosperous and even beautiful – a central focal point that the whole of Astria could be proud of.

Now, however, the shops that lined each side were dilapidated and had clearly seen better days. The stalls in the central market were half-empty and lacking in most of the basic goods. The few scared shoppers seemed desperate to get back to their homes as quickly as possible.

The grey weather didn't help things, but the entire place had a deathly pallor, as if the marsh's ghostly fogs had wrung the joy and life out of it.

'The people seem terrified,' Thea whispered.

Quinn nodded in agreement. One day, if he

defeated Vayn, he would be Emperor of this place, although he wondered if the Black Guard would have left anything behind for him to rule over.

'We should split up,' Ignus said, glancing around the market square. 'We're too conspicuous like this, and the Black Guard will have been told to keep an eye out for Quinn and Thea and myself.'

A group of Black Guard were beginning to gather at one side of the square.

'I need to find some magical supplies anyway,' Thea said. 'Come on, Quinn. You're with me.'

'The rest of us will look for somewhere to hole up,' Ignus said. 'Meet back here in an hour.'

'And I will take my leave,' Maria said. 'You kept your side of the bargain and helped me find my cousin and I've shown you the way across the swamp.'

'We're not finished,' Quinn promised her again. 'We'll find a way to save her. Somehow.'

He pressed his hands into hers and she said goodbye to each of the travellers in turn. 'Until we meet again.'

The Black Guard across the square had started to idle their way towards the group.

'C'mon,' Quinn hissed, grabbing Thea's arm. Together, they darted back into the winding streets, as Ulric, Ignus and Maria went in the opposite direction.

Quinn had never been in such a big town before. His village on Yaross had only had about fifty houses, and he'd known every single person living there. He guessed there must have been at least ten thousand people living here. The streets were a warren of twisting passages and high dark houses. How someone could find anything or anyone here, he had no idea. Thea didn't seem to have a much better idea, either. No one would stop to talk to them when they tried to ask for directions, and most of the shops they peered in were dark and locked up.

'This is pointless,' Quinn said as they turned into a rubbish-strewn alley. Everywhere he looked, people were poor and scared, and they were shooting angry, sullen glances at everyone they passed. That was what twelve years of Vayn's rule had done to Keriss.

'Watch out!' Thea hissed.

Quinn glanced up to see a patrol of Black Guard enter the far end of the alley. For a second, Quinn froze, but he and Thea were in plain sight, so they couldn't turn back.

'Hoods up,' he hissed to Thea, pulling his over his head.

Together, they made their way down the alley towards the guardsmen, Quinn gritting his teeth while he hoped their hoods would hide their faces. Thea pulled Quinn against the wall as the guardsmen stalked up to them. Quinn kept his face turned down and felt the guardsmen's gazes burning into him. He clenched his fists and dug his fingernails into the palms of his hands so hard he winced.

Walk on past, he thought desperately. *Walk on past.*

With a grunt, the nearest guardsman shoved by, almost knocking Quinn into a pile of rotting food. He stumbled and caught himself but kept his eyes down as the patrol moved on, laughing.

'Close call,' Thea hissed. 'C'mon.'

They came out of the alley onto another cobbled road. Washing was strung across the street between the houses.

'We're lost,' Thea said, hopelessly. 'We're never going to find a magic shop . . .'

'How about up there?' Quinn said. The far end of the street eventually opened out and Quinn could see crowds of people clustered together. At the end of it, an enormous, fortified barracks flying the Emperor Vayn's black fist flag loomed in the distance. Huge stone walls rose up; only small slits for windows – or an archer's arrow – broke up the monolithic structure.

'That must be where Lorimer lives. I'm sure Maria said something about a barracks in an old castle,' Thea said.

'Well, at least there are some signs of life up there,' Quinn said. 'Come on.'

As they reached the main road, the deserted streets and nervous citizens gave way to a huge crowd milling around. People were packed close, trying to catch a glimpse of something moving past, up towards the castle. Quinn and Thea rushed to the back of the crowd to get a closer look and soon saw the reason for the crush.

A group of sentries were parading through the square on tall horses, heading for the grand barracks. A dozen dark steeds made their way through the thronging crowds, shoving past the townspeople as if they weren't even there. In the centre of the group, a tall man on a warhorse rode steadily forward, a sneer twisting his face.

'Clear the way!' one of the sentries bellowed, using his horse to shove the townspeople aside. 'Move, scum!'

Suddenly, the quiet murmuring of the crowd found its voice. One woman pushed her way to the front, pulling her tattered velvet cloak around her. Lines of worry wrinkled her brow as she desperately started shouting, 'Help us!' she cried. 'Our people are getting lost in the marshes. You're supposed to be protecting us!'

At first the crowd seemed scared by her

dissent, but gradually murmurs of agreement began circulating among them.

'My son went out to scavenge in the marshes because there's no food,' the woman continued. 'He never came back. What are you going to do about it? You need to go out and find him!'

The sentries didn't reply. They just kept shoving their horses forward despite the desperate cries. The murmurs in the crowd were getting louder and angrier.

'It looks like there's going to be a riot,' Quinn muttered to Thea.

Thea nodded, and together they tried to edge back through the crowd that was pressing forward. 'The people of Astria have had enough of the Black Guard.'

'Lorimer!' the woman shouted. 'You need to do something!'

The pompous man in the centre of the group turned on hearing his name, and looked down at the woman with contempt. He was wearing black armour, but not like the guards'. Instead it was inlaid with gold so that it glittered in the sunlight. His helmet was decorated with purple plumage that stuck up from his head like a warning sign. Quinn could see a sliver of a grin crack his powdered face as he looked down his nose at the crowd. *Lorimer. The man himself.*

'Lorimer!' the woman shouted again. 'Answer me!'

The crowd went silent as Lorimer paused to consider the trembling woman below him.

'You dare speak to me?' he whispered, his thin, menacing voice carrying across the crowd like a toxic gas. Everyone seemed to be holding their breath in anticipation. 'Take her away . . .'

'No!' The woman cried, dodging back and merging with the crowd, as a Black Guard tried to grab her.

Lorimer raged as she slipped from his grasp. 'Catch her!' he growled. 'And beat these people back!'

The brutish sentries around him drew their swords and turned the butts of their spears on the crowds, lashing out at the men and women. The people were so packed together they couldn't turn and run. Quinn saw and heard wood thump into flesh.

Lorimer spurred his warhorse and it leapt forward, barrelling through the people.

The crowd surged. Quinn was knocked to the side, banging into Thea. He grabbed her by one arm to stop her falling. If they fell to the ground here, they would be crushed under the feet of the panicked townspeople.

The sentries moved forward, jabbing with spears and swiping with the flats of their swords. An elbow caught Quinn under his chin and he grunted in pain. He felt dragon scales form under his shirt.

At the front of the crowd, Quinn saw the woman who had been shouting at Lorimer go down as the crowd tried to get away from the advancing horses. The sentries didn't seem to care. They kept on pressing forward and the crowd stumbled away. The woman was being battered from all sides and she couldn't regain her feet.

'She'll be crushed!' he yelled, leaping forward. He shoved his way through the retreating crowd.

Bodies bounced into him, and he fell to his knees. He grabbed on to a man in front and hauled himself up.

Ahead of them, one of the sentries urged his horse forward. The woman tried to rise, but the press of the crowd knocked her back. The horse's hooves rose above her and she raised her arms up in terror, letting out a horrified shriek . . .

CHAPTER 9
A VOICE FROM AFAR

Quinn darted into the crowd and grabbed one of her arms, hauling her back. The horse whinnied as its hooves hit the cobbles with a smack.

A moment later, Thea joined Quinn, and together they dragged the woman out of the square and into a narrow alley. The sentries were dispersing the rest of the crowd, and townspeople were limping away as fast as they could, supporting each other. Quinn saw bloody faces and heard the laughs of the sentries as they cantered around the square on their horses.

'Thank you,' the woman said, breathlessly. She looked in pain, but she didn't seem badly injured. 'You didn't have to do that.'

'We couldn't leave you,' Quinn objected.

'All I wanted was for the town guard to do something about my son. He's been missing for over a week. I . . . I'm afraid for him. The Stone Trolls have been coming closer to Astria.' She glanced at the square. 'Lorimer does nothing to protect us . . .'

'We're going to help,' Quinn said fiercely. 'We'll find a way to overthrow the Black Guard and get rid of the Stone Trolls.'

Thea leaned over, frowning and peering at the woman's neck. The woman's hand went up self-consciously.

'What is it?' Quinn said.

'That necklace you're wearing . . .' Thea said. 'I recognise the symbol.'

The woman slowly pulled her hand away, revealing a rough piece of obsidian carved with what looked like a crane, its wings outstretched in flight.

'What if it is?' the woman said defensively. 'There's nothing illegal about magic.'

Quinn knew this was true, but he also knew that the Black Guard didn't like people practising magic. Thea was proof of that – she'd been cast off her home, the Rock of Sighs, when her tutor Telemus was teaching her sorcery. Black armour might be proof against any ordinary weapon, but the Guard could never be sure against magic.

'Oh, I know!' Thea grinned, happily. 'In fact you're just the kind of person I've been looking for.'

Quinn curled himself up into a warm velvet armchair, dry and comfortable for the first time in days. The woman they had saved, Mother Onyx, had invited them to stay. Having scoured the streets for Ignus and Ulric, they had eventually found them and brought them back to her small house. Quinn looked out of the window across the sloping roofs to the mist-covered mountains in the distance – the two Dragon

Knights were busying themselves by the fire and Thea was deep in conversation with Mother Onyx. The bottom room of her house was where she stocked dozens of mysterious potions, strange magical items, and what looked to Quinn like really unpleasant dried bits of animal. To Thea it looked like heaven – a magical treasure trove to rival all others.

'Do you really think you can help my son?' Mother Onyx asked anxiously, pushing back her bundle of grey hair from her lined face. She had wild, flashing, sea-green eyes, and an air of eccentricity and distraction. Quinn couldn't help but be reminded of his Aunt Marta.

'We're going to try,' Quinn said, firmly.

It wasn't just Mother Onyx's son or Maria's cousin. Dozens of people had been turned to rock by Vayn's Stone Trolls in the marshes. If he ever managed to overthrow Vayn, it would end, but in the meantime, people were disappearing every day. As long as the Black Guard held the only safe road and the Stone Trolls stalked the marshes, Quinn knew people would keep disappearing. The only way to stop it was by getting rid of the Guard *and* the Stone Trolls.

'That necklace,' Thea said to Mother Onyx. 'It's a symbol of Astrian magic, isn't it?'

Their host nodded. 'The seeing magic. All magic users in Astria carry the symbol. If you want to know why there's a city in the middle of the swamp, it's not just the mines in the mountains here, it's the old magic.'

'The symbol is called the magic wing,' Ulric commented from beside the fire. 'Because you can send messages on the air. I remember Vayn coming here to learn the secrets of the seeing magic. That was before he turned against your father, Quinn.'

'That's what I thought,' Thea said, nodding. 'Ever since I started studying magic, I've heard people talking about the Seeing Stones of Astria. They say the stones of Astria are the best in the Twelve Islands.'

'It's true,' Mother Onyx said. 'Their secrets have been passed down from mother to daughter for hundreds of years.'

'You know how to make them?' Thea said, leaning forward eagerly, her eyes flashing with wonder. 'Only I've been looking for something.' She glanced over at Quinn. He frowned, wondering what she was looking at him like that for.

'Not me,' the older woman said, with a smile. 'I'm only a dealer in magical items. I don't have that kind of magic talent.'

'Seeing stone?' Quinn interrupted. He'd never heard of them. But then his Aunt Marta had been the only person Quinn had ever known who possessed magic, until he'd met Thea.

'They allow people to see across great distances,' Mother Onyx said. 'If you know the right charms, you can even talk to others who are also in possession of a seeing stone. An Astrian Seeing Stone is a remarkably powerful item and far too valuable for a trader like me to be selling.'

Thea's face dropped. 'Oh.'

'But I do have one of my own,' Mother Onyx said with a mischievous grin. 'I inherited it.'

Thea brightened again. 'Can we borrow it?'

Mother Onyx nodded and got up.

'You're going to like this,' Thea promised Quinn. 'If it works . . .'

Mother Onyx disappeared into her bedroom, then returned a minute later carrying a very large and heavy round stone cupped in her hands. She laid it on her low table. Quinn peered at it. Streaks of different colours flashed through it, forming complex, twisting patterns on the surface. Hundreds of tiny runes had been carved into the stone.

'I used to use it to contact my son,' Mother Onyx said, 'but I can't any more. That's how I know something has happened to him.'

'Can I?' Thea asked, indicating the stone.

'Of course,' Mother Onyx said.

Thea beckoned Quinn over. He uncurled from his chair, frowning. Suddenly he knew what Thea was up to.

Thea placed her hands on either side of the stone and muttered a spell under her breath. Nothing happened. Quinn looked across at her, quizzically.

'It needs the breath of life,' Mother Onyx whispered.

Thea fell back into deep concentration, her red hair falling across her shoulders, forming a curtain round her face. She tried once more to spark the stone into life, muttering a spell under her breath. This time she breathed on it, gently, and the seeing stone began to glow. Colours danced around it, chasing the patterns in the stone, swirling faster and faster and pulsing with an otherworldly light.

With Thea deep in a trance, there was only one word Quinn could make out: *Marta*.

Then an ethereal figure crept into existence, foggy and distant in the stone.

Quinn gasped.

She stared right at him, her eyes wide. The seeing stone pulsed with magical energy, sending out multi-coloured rays of light into the room.

Marta had been holding her sewing in one hand, but now she let it fall unnoticed on her lap.

'Quinn?' she said. Her voice seemed to echo around the room as clearly as if she'd been standing right there in front of him. He felt if he reached out to touch the stone, he'd be able to touch her face.

'That's good spell-casting,' Mother Onyx murmured. 'You're a natural . . .'

Thea remained silent, caught in the magic, trying to hold onto the spell.

'Are you all right?' Quinn cried urgently to his aunt. He'd been desperately trying not to worry about her, but he hadn't been able to stop thinking about her being locked in a dungeon somewhere on Yaross Island.

She didn't look like she was in a dungeon, or in trouble. Quinn could make out a window behind her showing a bright blue sky with high, fast clouds and a glint of distant water beneath it. She wasn't dressed in the shapeless, brown outfit she'd always worn at home either, but in a proper gown. For the first time, Quinn could actually imagine her as a lady of the Emperor's court.

'My boy,' she said, her voice ringing with joy. 'I'm well. I am with a friend – an old lady of the court.'

Quinn sighed with relief.

Marta continued. 'It would be best if I didn't say where I am. The Guard will be looking for me, just like they are looking for you.' She leaned forward. 'I heard what you did on Yaross Island. Your father would be proud.'

Quinn felt himself blush.

'Where are you?' Marta said.

Quinn cleared his throat. 'Keriss.'

Marta's face darkened. 'I wish you could have avoided that place,' she whispered.

Quinn knew exactly what Marta was thinking.

'That's what I need to ask you,' Quinn said. 'My parents – what really happened to them?'

'Are you sure you want to know?' Marta said, carefully.

'Yes,' Quinn said, even though it was the last thing he wanted to think about. 'I have to . . .'

Marta nodded. 'Their ship did go down near the coast, just as I told you, but it wasn't an accident. Vayn ordered one of his minions to plant an explosive on board. It went off just as it was approaching the harbour. No one had a chance in those waters – not in the Kerissian Pass.'

Quinn remembered the razor-sharp rocks that jutted from the sea like a dragon's snapping jaw.

'But my father was a dragonblood,' Quinn said.

'They're hard to kill,' Marta whispered, 'but not invincible. Your father must have been killed before he had a chance to transform . . .'

Quinn felt the helpless rage building up in him again, like a mist descending upon him. He felt the dragonblood course through his veins, hot and angry.

'Do . . . do you know what the killer was called?' he managed. He hardly recognised his own voice.

Marta sighed. 'I do. He went by the name of Lorimer.'

CHAPTER 10

THE HEAT OF THE MOMENT

Marta might have said more, but if so, Quinn didn't hear it. It was as if there was fire raging in his ears. *That* was what Lorimer had done for Vayn – that was why he was flouncing through Astria, treating it like his own personal citadel. He had murdered the Emperor and Empress. He had murdered Quinn's own parents, and he'd been rewarded for it. Vayn had given him Keriss Island as payment, to treat as his own kingdom.

Quinn felt his hands clenching into fists. The ends of his fingers itched as talons pressed against the inside of his skin. Scales burst out over his chest, turning it hard and golden. He could feel his dragonform demanding to be released, and he wanted to set it free.

He leapt to his feet and made for the door.

'Quinn, what are you doing?' Thea cried, but Quinn ignored her. Ignus and Ulric called out too, but he was already jumping down the stairs five at a time. He heard the others dash down behind him – but not fast enough. The dragon inside him was seething like the tides around Keriss Island.

Lorimer! The man thought he was a king. He thought he could murder the Emperor and Empress and get away with it. Quinn was going to show him otherwise. Screaming his anger, he rushed away through the streets, heading towards the steep walls of Lorimer's castle, throwing away his caution. He heard Ignus's deep booming in the distance, but darted round alleyways faster than the flame dragon could follow.

The cobbled roads were mostly empty as darkness fell over the town. Quinn guessed that most of the Astrian citizens were holed up for the night, keeping out of the way of the Black Guard. Only a few small groups of people huddled in doorways or staggered out from taverns.

There were guardsmen standing at the doors of the great, fortified barracks, and other small groups of guardsmen patrolling around the walls. Quinn didn't have a plan, but the dragon force inside him was driving him forward. There was no turning back now . . .

The old castle's doors were made of solid oak and framed by stone pillars. Four guardsmen stood directly in front of them. The yellow light of the flaming torches above them flickered on their armour.

'Halt!' the first guard cried.

'Out of my way!' Quinn shouted as he approached. 'I'm going in.' Fury was bouncing around inside him like a tiger batting at the bars of a cage.

The guardsmen looked at each other, then burst into sudden laughter.

'Get out of here, boy,' one of them called, 'before we beat you bloody.'

Quinn's dragonform came surging forward.

Beat me bloody? Quinn could scarcely contain his anger. His eyes started to glow a burning gold as the dragonform grew inside him. He snatched the golden sword from its scabbard and stalked towards the guardsmen.

'I will speak to Lorimer,' he cried.

Suddenly the disbelieving laughter slipped from the guard's face. Instead, he looked deadly serious.

'You should watch what you say, boy,' he said, drawing his weapon.

Suddenly, as if a light bulb had switched off in his mind, Quinn's resolve faltered. The dragonblood dimmed, and instead of being blinded by rage, he became all too aware of the dangerous situation he'd put himself in. *What am I doing here?*

He felt the dragonform stutter inside him and retreat as doubt dampened his anger. The scales under his shirt started to fade.

Uh oh! Quinn realised his mistake.

The first guardsman lifted a double-handed

blade. It looked big enough to cut Quinn cleanly in two. He raised his own golden sword.

The guardsman swung lazily at Quinn, as though he thought Quinn was hardly worth bothering with. Quinn leapt back and deflected the sword. He swung his own sword and the guardsman stumbled, scrabbling just out of range. Quinn could have followed it up and run the man through, but the other guardsmen closed in, slashing at him. Quinn threw himself back, tumbling across the cobbles. The guardsmen lunged after him, and Quinn rolled again, throwing himself just out of reach.

Suddenly, a scream sounded, high and piercing, to the west of the castle walls. Then another scream and shouts followed it.

Quinn looked around and let his sword fall to his side.

Something vast and dark emerged from a side street, big and heavy enough to shake the ground beneath it and send the guardsmen staggering back. Its huge grey head looked like a boulder perched on a mountain. Its yellow eyes burned with a dumb, unthinking rage, and a glint of dark magic. Muscles rippled across its barrel of a belly, and a fine dust came off it as it shook with anger. As it stepped into the torchlight, Quinn saw it for what it was.

'By gods!' one of the guards murmured.

Barging its way up the road towards the castle doors, a giant Kerissian Stone Troll lumbered straight at Quinn. With a deep howl, which exposed teeth like forgotten gravestones, the troll put its head down and charged.

Cobblestones cracked under its feet as it slammed across the road, picking up speed. Just one touch would turn him into a stone statue, Quinn remembered, just like those poor souls petrified in the marshes.

'Argh!' he yelled, throwing himself to one side. His shoulder hit the hard ground with a jolt that made his teeth rattle and his vision swim. He rolled on the ground, feeling himself pick up bruises as he went. He stopped just behind a lamp, and desperately tried to hide himself.

Guardsmen raced in across the square as the alarm was raised. The troll charged towards the guards on the main gate, smashing into them and roaring with rage. The guards fought back, pounding the troll with their magically strengthened swords. It fell back, howling, and crashed into the gas lamp where Quinn was cowering.

The troll twisted in pain, and locked eyes with Quinn, who prepared to be turned to stone or smashed into a bloody pulp, but instead, there was a flicker of recognition between them . . .

'Get away,' it hissed, as if speaking through gravel. 'Run!'

Quinn scrambled to his feet, his mind racing . . . *Was that . . . Ulric?*

More guardsmen were pelting across the road towards them. The Stone Troll fought against them, but the guards began to organise as the surprise of the troll's attack faltered. Quinn watched in horror as an approaching group of guardsmen tossed a net over the troll and dragged it down. It crashed to the ground not ten feet from Quinn. Another net followed, entangling the troll further, and guardsmen closed in, weapons raised.

'No!' Quinn hissed.

Suddenly, the Stone Troll didn't look so large or so fierce any more. Ulric couldn't sustain the illusion, not for this long. The stone body was slipping away, revealing clothes and skin and hair, and a familiar moustache.

From across the road he made eye contact with the Dragon Knight, whose eyes pleaded with Quinn. He was giving him a chance . . . he was telling him, 'Get out of here.'

One of the guardsmen let out a shout of delight. He tugged at the nets and grabbed Ulric by one arm, hauling the scrawny man to his feet. Ulric looked small and bedraggled surrounded by the armoured guards.

The guardsman holding Ulric turned and addressed some citizens, who were suddenly gathering round.

'This is the dragonblood who has been terrorising the city. This is the man who is responsible for your family members going missing in the marshes. We have caught him, and he will face justice for what he has done to you!'

And for the first time that he could remember, Quinn heard the ordinary people of the Twelve Islands cheering the Black Guard.

Quinn knew he had no choice but to turn and flee.

CHAPTER 11

A NEW PLAN

Quinn flung back the sheets and rolled out of bed. The sweat dripped from his forehead as he pushed away memories of the nightmare. Except it wasn't a bad dream – the night before came flooding back to him. The loss of control, the ridiculous attempt to storm the fortress . . .

He'd met Ignus and Thea on the way back to Mother Onyx's and told them what had happened. When he did, Ignus had looked so disappointed in him he could barely look him in the eye.

And you want to be Emperor, he asked himself. *What kind of Emperor acts like that?*

Wincing, he made his way into Mother Onyx's dining room. Thea and Ignus were already up, eating breakfast. Neither of them looked at him when he came in.

Awkwardly, Quinn cleared his throat. 'I know I made a mistake,' he said.

Thea looked up and smiled, but Ignus remained quiet, throwing a glance from under his thick brows. The silence hung heavy in the air.

Quinn's voice was so quiet he could hardly hear it himself. 'I'm sorry.'

'You're sorry?' Ignus bellowed. 'That's it?'

Thea laid a hand on Ignus's arm to calm him.

Quinn hung his head. 'Yes.' He looked back up, eyes blazing. 'I was wrong about Ulric. I should have trusted him. I should have knighted him and released him from Vayn's shackles.' If he had, he knew Ulric wouldn't have been captured. 'I'll free him – I'll get him out of there!' he practically yelled.

'And how are you going to do that?' Ignus barked.

'I have an idea,' Quinn began, 'but I need both of you to help. . .'

Thea nodded but Ignus looked up at him warily and a huffed a reply. 'I hope this idea's a good one . . .'

Two days later, Mother Onyx led them to the castle. The previous night's mist was still hanging over the town and curling through the streets in thin tendrils, waiting for the sun to burn it away. A few people were out and about, heading for work or pushing barrows of supplies towards the market. Quinn and the others kept their heads down as they hurried past.

The prison was to the west of the castle, where the stone walls began to merge into the surrounding rock. A small entry point was carved into the sandstone.

'Are you sure about this?' Thea said, as they approached.

Quinn nodded. 'I don't see that there's any other way.'

'Here, take this,' Mother Onyx whispered,

slipping a small stone charm into Quinn's hand. 'And remember what I told you.' She handed Quinn a basket of old bread and hard, stale cheese. He was glad Ulric wasn't going to have to eat any of it.

'Wish me luck,' he said.

'I'll wish you a lack of stupidity,' muttered Ignus, who was still acting like a dragon with a sore head.

Quinn straightened. Leaving the others at the corner of the street, he walked up to the prison entrance. A stained, wooden door with a small, barred window led into the solid block of the prison. One of the sentries held up a hand as Quinn approached.

'What's your business?' the man said.

Quinn put on an ingratiating smile and tightly clasped the charm in his hand.

'My uncle was arrested two days ago,' Quinn said. 'I've brought him some food.'

'Let me see,' the sentry demanded.

Quinn held out the basket with both hands. As the guard took it, Quinn gently touched his wrist.

'*Igresias Artu*,' he whispered.

A spark jolted between them and the guard's eyes glazed over. With the power of Mother Onyx's charm and the spell Thea had placed on it, Quinn got to work on the guard's mind.

'I'd just like to get past,' he suggested.

'*You'd just like to get past*,' the guard said, hazily.

'And you're going to let me.'

'*And I'm going to let you.*'

Another sentry came forward and began to pat Quinn down roughly – but found nothing. Quinn was one step ahead of them.

'Nothing, sir,' the second sentry said. He peered at the food too. 'Not even anything worth stealing.' He shoved the basket back to Quinn.

Quinn didn't say anything. He just stood there, staring down at his feet, trying to look harmless.

'So I can go in . . .' he murmured.

'*You can go in*,' the first sentry said, pulling open the door and shoving Quinn through.

There were two more sentries sitting at a table inside, but they just nodded towards a dark stairway behind them that led downward. Quinn boldly headed past them and started down the stairs. He felt a thrill course through him . . . *It had worked*. He slipped the stone into his pocket, and made his way down.

The stairs were carved out of the bare rock of the valley that the town sat in. The walls were wet and it was slippery underfoot. Quinn had to reach out one hand to stop himself falling. He could feel the cold and damp radiating from the walls and the only light came from the torches flickering on the walls. Quinn felt the guilt creep across him – he'd practically sent Ulric here.

At last the stairway opened onto a narrow hallway. A torch burned at the far end. It gave off more smoke than light or warmth, but it was enough for Quinn to see a dozen cells with thick iron bars across their entrances. The cells themselves had been hacked out of solid rock.

Most of the cells were empty, but Quinn soon found Ulric slumped against the wall of the furthest one. The Dragon Knight looked terrible. The Black Guard had obviously beaten him when he'd been arrested and the cold and damp of the cell had turned his skin an unhealthy white. But he struggled up and crossed to the cell door when Quinn appeared.

'What are you doing here?' Ulric hissed. He peered over Quinn's shoulder at the empty hallway. 'You must be mad! If they recognise you . . .'

'I've come to get you out of here,' Quinn said. 'And to apologise. I should have trusted you. I was just . . .' He remembered how terrified he'd been when Ulric had loomed over him in the guise of the horned highwayman. 'I was embarrassed. I treated you badly but you still showed me loyalty. Now you're locked up in here and it's my fault.'

Ulric looked at him gravely. 'You are the true Emperor. I swore my life to protect you and your family. I could not save your parents, but I could save you.' He looked around again. 'You should not have come.'

'I'm not like Vayn,' Quinn said. 'I wouldn't leave you down here. If I had control of my dragon abilities . . .'

'I know you've been having trouble with your dragonform,' Ulric said. 'It doesn't always come easily, and Ignus is no help to anyone. I never saw anyone transform into a dragon so easily. It's probably because he's got such a bad temper.' Ulric laughed.

Quinn could agree with that.

'And flame dragons are simpler souls,' Ulric continued. 'They come from the original line of Dragon Knights from eons ago. All dragons can breathe *some* fire, but theirs is the most devastating. Over the years, other dragons have emerged, like me, with all sorts of abilities.'

'So you think I might not just be a flame dragon then?' Quinn asked.

'I doubt it.' Ulric said. 'You wouldn't be having so much trouble if there wasn't something special about your form. Take a bit of advice from someone who took years to learn how to do it properly: use your emotions rather than fighting against them. Let them flow, and you'll transform, I promise you.'

Quinn felt better for this. At least when he

became a dragon, he would have something more than flames to look forward to. He reached into the basket, pushing the mouldy food out of the way, and drew out the jade-handled knife hidden there. As he took it in his hand, it transformed into his father's golden sword, glowing softly in the dim light of the cells.

'Kneel,' Quinn said.

Ulric cleared his throat. 'It would be an honour to serve the Emperor once more . . .'

Quinn reached through the bars and laid the flat of the blade on Ulric's shoulder. Just as it had when he'd knighted Ignus, the sword began to glow brighter and brighter until the golden light turned the cell as bright as day. Something ancient and powerful stirred inside him and, unbidden, the ancient language of the dragons emerged from his lips.

'By the power of dragonblood and in the sight of the gods, I bind you to protect the Twelve Islands against all threat and I bind your loyalty to the true Emperor. Advance, Ulric, Dragon Knight of the Twelve Islands.'

A crack sounded, echoing from the cell walls, and the manacles binding Ulric's ankles shattered. Purple fire burned across them and then was gone.

Slowly, Ulric straightened. 'At last, my friend,' he whispered. He rolled his shoulders. 'I have been waiting to do this for twelve long years.'

The Dragon Knight's eyes began to glow, and Quinn saw emerald green scales appear on his neck and hands.

'Umm. . . Isn't your cell a little small?' Quinn asked urgently.

Ulric winked at him. 'Watch and learn.'

The Dragon Knight bent over, wings springing from his back and unfolding like a ship's sails. His body grew rapidly, swelling and changing, becoming long and scaly. His arms and legs twisted and razor-sharp claws jutted from his fingers, bending themselves into talons. A tail whipped out, cracking against the rock walls. Still Ulric grew fast until his wings brushed the top of the cell.

'Ride your emotions to change,' the Shadow

Dragon said, in a low, rumbling voice, 'but know when to get off. That's something Ignus has never learnt. It's all a bit too subtle for him. Now, stand back.'

Quinn stumbled away from the cell door. With a growl, the Shadow Dragon lashed out with one leg. Dragon claws smashed into metal, and with a shriek, the iron bars tore. The door ripped from the stone and fell with a clatter to the floor. Ulric's long neck snaked out. He turned towards the hallway and stairs and sent a blast of steam racing along it. 'That's better,' he said. 'I've needed to clear my throat properly for years.'

Quinn heard a clanging of armour and weaponry from above. 'You know,' he said. 'I was planning on a quieter escape than this.'

The dragon appeared to shrug, and within moments, Ulric's dragonform had fallen away, leaving Ulric standing there, straightening his clothes.

'Don't worry. I'll cloud the minds of the sentries.' He winked. 'One of the advantages of being a Shadow Dragon. People see and hear what I want them to.'

'And you wonder why people don't trust you,' Quinn muttered.

Carefully, Quinn and Ulric crept up the dark steps towards the faint light from the guardroom above. Quinn felt his stomach tensing and it was all he could do not to curl his hands into painful fists. Ulric hardly seemed bothered. He was striding up, humming loudly to himself. *At least someone's confident of their powers*, Quinn thought, gratefully.

The sentries in the guardroom were drawing their swords just as Ulric and Quinn emerged from the stairwell. Quinn gritted his teeth and his hand dropped to his own blade. It looked like they were going to have to fight their way out. But then Quinn looked down as his body seemed to shift from under him.

Suddenly, the guards sheathed their swords and saluted.

'Lord Lorimer!' one of them stammered. 'We had no idea you were down there.'

Ulric raised his eyebrow. 'Is that what you call doing your job?'

The men backed away. 'No, sir. Sorry, sir. But . . .'

'Can we just get out of here?' Quinn hissed in Ulric's ear.

'Spoilsport,' Ulric whispered.

'Come *on*.'

With a loud sigh, Ulric turned back to the shivering guards. 'I will be returning. If I *ever* find you paying so little attention to your duties again, I'll nail your heads to the city walls. Understand?'

Ulric followed Quinn out of the prison, between the two sentries outside the door, who almost dropped their spears at the sight of them.

'You might have warned me you were going to disguise us as Black Guardsmen,' Quinn grated through gritted teeth.

'Where would be the fun in that?' Ulric said.

It might have been cold in the cells, but Quinn was now sweating madly. All he wanted to do was to break into a run and dash down the street, away from the prison. But he didn't know how far Ulric's magic would stretch, so he forced himself to take slow, calm steps as they walked down the street.

When they reached the end, Ulric turned to Quinn with a grin. 'And that, Your Imperial Majesty, is how you do an escape. I thank you.'

Quinn felt a flutter as Ulric's magic dropped away.

'Not too rusty, if I do say so myself,' the Shadow Dragon mused.

But he spoke too soon. A cry sounded from the prison at the far end of the street. Quinn whirled around. The sentries had been keeping a better lookout than he'd realised. Now one of them was pointing directly at Quinn and Ulric. Even as Quinn watched, more sentries came racing around the side of the prison and pounded down the street towards them, weapons drawn.

CHAPTER 12

THE GOLDEN DRAGON

'Halt! Stop them!' the guards cried.

Quinn turned and raced down the street, away from the prison, Ulric sprinting after him.

'Run,' he hissed.

'I am!' Ulric panted.

They were meant to meet Thea and Ignus at the far end of the street, but the guards would be on him and Ulric before they could reach them.

Quinn glanced around. Ulric was a good ten paces behind and the sentries were closing in fast.

A man stepped out of a side street, pulling a heavily-laden handcart behind him. There was no time to dodge. Quinn leapt, but his foot caught on the cart, sending him flying. He crashed into a group of people, who went tumbling, and hauled himself up before they could react. He sprinted on, ignoring the angry yells behind.

Quinn felt a stitch burning in his side. Every breath felt like he was sucking in red hot embers from a fire. He glanced back again. The guards were gaining ground, using their drawn weapons to scatter the crowds while Quinn had to dodge and dart between people.

He bounced off a big man carrying a sack and almost lost his footing.

We'll have to fight, Quinn thought. He slowed and reached for his sword. *It's time I put this to use.*

But the shadow dragon had other ideas.

'Now!' Ulric hissed. The Dragon Knight put on a burst of speed, grabbed Quinn by the arm and hauled him into a dense crowd. They ducked down behind a stall and Quinn felt Ulric's magic sweep over him again at the Dragon Knight's touch. Quinn felt himself shrink down and his back hunch over. The next moment, he and Ulric, bent like beggar women, hobbled out into the street.

The guards sprinted straight at them, swords drawn . . .

And kept on running. Grinning, Ulric let go of Quinn, and the 'shadow magic', and led the way to the side alley where Thea and Ignus were waiting.

'Nice move!' Quinn gasped, clutching his side.

Ulric looked smug. 'As far as they're concerned, we've disappeared off in the other direction.'

'You shouldn't have let them see you,' Ignus rumbled. 'They'll be looking for us now. The whole of the Black Guard will be out in force.'

'Did I ever tell you you're no fun, Ignus?' Ulric said.

Ignus loomed over the smaller Dragon Knight. 'This isn't about *fun*. This is about taking the Twelve Islands back from Vayn and freeing our people. If you ever endanger the Emperor's life like that again, I'll tear off your arms and shove them down your throat. Understand?'

Thea inserted herself between them. 'Stop arguing, you two! The Black Guard know we're here now. We need to get out of town. Your magic might be powerful, Ulric, but even you can't keep it up forever. Unless you want to get into a fight with the whole of the Astrian Black Guard?'

'We're not ready for that,' Ignus growled, glaring at Ulric. 'If we're going to take on the Guard and Vayn, we need to do it on our terms with our full strength. Not because some idiot gets us caught.'

'Then let's move,' Quinn said. 'It won't take the sentries long to realise they've lost us. They'll close the town gates and we'll be trapped.'

Quinn, Ignus, Thea and Ulric hurried through the streets, watching out for Black Guardsmen and sentries. Twice they had to hide in doorways as guardsmen crossed the street ahead of them. It became increasingly difficult to move unnoticed as more and more citizens emerged from their houses. Ulric used his abilities sparingly – disappearing in front of ordinary townspeople would cause uproar and bring the Guard right to them.

At last, though, the town wall came into sight. The massive, iron-studded wooden gates stood ajar, and a few townspeople were making their way out, no doubt to work on farms or gather wood on the edges of the marshes, outside the safety of the town. Quinn didn't envy them. The Stone Trolls would still be out there. If Ulric's illusion was anything to go by, they were terrifying creatures.

'Ready?' he whispered.

The others nodded.

'Don't stop,' Ulric said. 'Stay calm and walk out like it's nothing in the world.'

With a deep breath, Quinn stepped out from the shelter of a house and walked casually towards the gate. He heard the others follow behind him, not crowding too close so as not to make them all look suspicious. The guardsmen on the gate were glancing at the people leaving the city, but no one was being searched or questioned. Quinn's heart started to thump. *Word must not have got out to the gate guardsmen yet*, he thought.

We're going to do it! It was all he could do not to break into a run.

Suddenly, the sound of horses' hooves rattled along the cobblestones. Quinn's head snapped up.

From around the side of a large turret, a troop of Black Guard rode out and formed a line across the gate. At their head, Quinn recognised the pompous figure of Lorimer. The man smirked down at Quinn and the others. He had twenty men with him, and they'd all drawn their weapons.

'Halt!' he cried, putting a hand to his sword.

'Get out of here,' Ignus shouted, bullying his way forward.

Quinn spun desperately, looking for a side street they could dash down, but before he could move, more Black Guard and town guard swarmed from every alley and street around them.

'There's nowhere to go!' Thea said.

Within moments, dozens upon dozens of armed men surrounded them.

Quinn glared up at Lorimer. Just the sight of the man who had murdered his parents sent his blood boiling inside his veins. He wanted to roar and rip him apart.

'And where exactly,' Lorimer drawled, 'do you think you're going with my prisoner?'

Quinn's blood boiled. He knew he should try to bluff and wait until he got his chance. After all, Lorimer couldn't know about Thea's magic or who Ignus was. The moment Lorimer dropped his guard they could act.

But Quinn couldn't stop himself. Lorimer had *murdered his parents.*

'I am leaving town,' Quinn ground out. 'With *my knight.*'

Lorimer's eyes widened, then he let out a delighted laugh. 'You're the one Lord Vayn told us to look out for! This is like every holy day come at once. My reward will be great.'

'And you're the one who destroyed the ship carrying the real Emperor and Empress!' Quinn spat. The fury building up inside him was making him shake.

'I'd do it again for the glory of the Emperor Vayn,' Lorimer gloated. 'It was so easy. The fools never knew what hit them. A Dragon Knight! It didn't stop him being blown to pieces, did it? My only regret is that he died before he could drown like your mother.'

Fury exploded in Quinn like a volcano erupting. He couldn't control it. It raged through every cell in his body, burning him up.

Ride it, Ulric had said. Use it. Don't fight it.

With a fierce pleasure, Quinn let the anger carry him. He didn't try to control it. It was like riding a great wave with only a thin plank under him. At any moment it might engulf him and drag him down, but it didn't. He kept on skimming over it, letting it take him onward.

He felt his body start to change. His skin hardened and his back bent. Claws erupted from his fingertips and toes. His neck lengthened and his spine burst from the small of his back as a tail twisted out. His bones felt like they were breaking. He could sense the organs in his body stretching, bursting and reforming. It was agony, but Quinn didn't care, because the power was gathering in him and it felt unreal. The skin above his shoulder blades split with a tearing sound that reverberated all the way to his feet, and wings burst out behind him.

His eyesight was better than it had ever been, and he could hear the blood rushing through the veins of the men around him, their pulses racing in panic. He smelled the fear on their skin.

He saw Thea's mouth drop open in shock and amazement and a fierce glare of delight spring across Ignus's face.

His body was coated in shining golden scales, and he towered as high as the houses. He tipped back his head and roared. He saw slates shaken loose from the surrounding houses fall and shatter on the cobblestones.

He bent his mighty legs, thrust, beat his gigantic wings, then launched himself into the clear sky.

CHAPTER 13

FLYING HIGH

Within seconds, Astria had fallen away beneath Quinn.

He beat his wings powerfully – the air gliding smoothly over his scales, lifting him high into the cloudless sky. He arched his back and dived and whirled across the air, spinning and turning and tracing great loops. The sensation was incredible – unlike anything he could have imagined. It was as natural as walking and just as easy. It was as if he'd spent his life lying in bed and suddenly discovered he could run.

Looking down through his dragon eyes he saw

Astria like a tiny cluster of children's building blocks squeezed into a toy valley, the whole of the mist-clung marshes and the stormy seas past Port Keriss. It would be easy to fly out over it. He could glide on the winds, scarcely needing to beat his wings. He opened his mouth and screamed a dragon-cry over the island.

This was what it was to be a dragonblood. No wonder Vayn had been jealous of his brother Marek.

The thought of Vayn brought him back. He'd left the others on the ground, surrounded by the Black Guard. It was time to fight – not try out his new skills.

Quinn folded his wings and plunged down, slicing through the sky like a living arrow. He saw tiny black figures look up from the ground, and he let out a scream that echoed across the sky.

He accelerated towards the ground and abruptly pulled himself back at the last minute, wings cracking like a whip as he shot across the heads of the guardsmen.

'Attack!' he bellowed towards the blurry figures of Thea, Ignus and Ulric.

With his new, razor-sharp claws, he reached out and snatched a Black Guardsman from his horse. He felt the supposedly impenetrable armour crack under the immense power of his talons. He let go of the guard and sent him flying over the roofs to crash onto the stones of the streets beyond.

Behind him, he felt two other dragons lift up to join him. A flash of bright white light crashed across the street as Thea cast a spell. Quinn glanced back to see her racing for cover as guardsmen covered their eyes in pain.

'Scatter them!' Ignus roared. 'They can't fight if they're not together.'

Quinn saw Ignus turn and go swooping back, a red flash of wings tearing through the sky. Fire erupted from his mouth, burning in a gigantic lance over the Black Guard. Several fell, but others raised magical shields to turn back the flame.

A squad of Black Guard stepped out from the

shelter of a building, raising bows. A flight of arrows scythed up, rising far higher than an arrow had any right to do.

Magic arrows! Quinn realised. He'd seen them at the Black Guard barracks back on Yaross Island.

He twisted and dived to the side as the flight of arrows whistled past him.

'Get higher!' he yelled to Ulric and Ignus, as the arrows magically returned to the guardsmen's hands, ready to be fired again.

His wings felt like they were burning as he fought against gravity, forcing himself higher and higher. He knew that even the magic arrows couldn't shoot up forever. Another arrow whipped past him, almost grazing his neck, but then he flew out of range.

He looked down in time to see Thea, who was crouched behind a water barrel, cast another spell that knocked the legs out from under the archers.

This is our chance!

He tucked his wings close against his body and dropped, feeling gravity take him. He angled himself towards the fight, then felt magic tickling over his scales. He glanced behind to see Ulric following him, emerald green scales glittering in the early morning light. Even as he looked, Quinn saw Ulric start to glow and he realised that he was glowing too, growing brighter and brighter as he plunged towards the Black Guard.

Light burned from Quinn's scales as Ulric's shadow magic surrounded him. Below, guardsmen covered their eyes against the blinding glare of the two plunging dragons. Quinn let out a deafening roar that sent guardsmen staggering back, deafened and unable to see. Soon, it would be Lorimer's turn.

Behind her water barrel, Thea rose up and began chanting, her hands moving in complex, weaving gestures, gathering her power. Then she thrust her hands forward. The air seemed to ripple then punch outwards. Guardsmen went scattering across the street, bouncing off walls and staggering helplessly to their feet again.

Then Quinn was among them. His claws smashed a pair of dazed guardsmen from their feet, the black armour shattering under the force of the blow. His massive tail whipped behind him, crushing a small group of guardsmen who had been taking shelter behind an overturned wagon. Another guardsman galloped out of a side street, swinging a sword in a great overhand blow. Quinn knocked the man contemptuously aside. Behind him, he heard the roar of Ignus's flame as the fire dragon joined the assault.

Quinn flapped up into the air again, feeling a fierce happiness. At last he was fighting back! Now to find Lorimer and finish this.

But then, something snatched at his left wing. He felt a sharp pain, like a red-hot needle jabbing into his skin. Arching his long, golden neck around, he saw an arrow lodged in the leathery underside, just behind the joint. His wing spasmed and suddenly Quinn lost control. He tried to flap with his one working wing, but the ease with which he'd controlled it just moments earlier had gone. Spinning helplessly, he was flung head first downwards, straight onto the street below . . .

CHAPTER 14
ESCAPE

Quinn let out a cry as his full weight smashed down into a house.

The impact was like being kicked in the chest by a horse. Tiles shattered and the roof beams smashed into splinters. Stones exploded outwards as the walls gave way under the enormous blow. The house fell to pieces as Quinn crunched downward through two floors.

He landed in the rubble, dazed, his head spinning. Every inch of his body flared in agony. He staggered to his feet and tried to peer through the dusty air. Splintered wood and cracked stone jutted up around him.

'No!' he cried, looking downwards. Instead of the golden scales and strong dragon muscles, he saw his usual human form, dressed in his ragged clothes. He'd been so busy plummeting to earth, his concentration had gone – he'd let go of his dragonform as he'd hit the ground. He patted his side and breathed a sigh of relief as he found his sword still there.

In the broken doorway of the house, two black-armoured figures loomed large, crunching through the debris.

'In here!' one of the guardsmen shouted.

Transform! Quinn thought frantically. He tried to find that anger and ride it again, but his head was spinning and he could hardly think straight.

Come on!

It was no good. His body was in too much pain and he stumbled away. With a shout, the guardsmen came charging in pursuit.

There was a back door to the destroyed house, but it was half full of rubble. Quinn flung himself onto it and scrambled up, trying to ignore the flaring pains in his back and head, and the dust in his mouth and nose. He coughed and staggered on.

The first guardsman swung at him and Quinn leapt forward. He clambered up the hillock of loose stone and rubble, slid down the other side and out of the door.

'Get back here!' the guardsman yelled.

No chance! Quinn thought, as he jumped to his feet and ran.

He burst out onto the main street and saw the chaos of the fight unfolding. Guardsmen were slumped against walls while others desperately tried to regroup. The street was full of smoke, and small fires burned everywhere from Ignus's burst of flame.

Up ahead, he saw Thea slip through the gates behind the Black Guard. Quinn put his head down and sprinted after her.

A guardsman saw him and shouted a warning,

but then Ignus came sweeping down, his fiery breath burning a furnace-hot line down the street, and the guardsmen had to crouch down behind their magical shields again.

'Go!' Ignus cried.

Quinn raced through the gate. Guardsmen came pounding in pursuit. Quinn's breath felt like fire in his chest.

Thea was waiting just past the gate. As Quinn ran through, she cast another spell and thick smoke billowed up behind him. He heard guardsmen coughing and choking as they plunged into it, but Quinn knew it wouldn't hold them forever.

'Go!' he shouted. 'Go!'

'This way!' Thea beckoned, then ran ahead of him down the sloping road towards the marshes.

'There'll be Black Guard on the main road,' Quinn panted. He could hardly get the words out he was so short of breath.

'Into the marshes again . . .' Thea managed in reply.

They reached the point in the road where they'd climbed out of the marshes, and leapt back off the dirt road, onto the soft, wet grass. As the mist crept about their legs, Quinn glanced back and saw the guardsmen emerge from the smoke and plunge after them in pursuit.

Ignus and Ulric appeared over the top of the walls, sending fire after the guardsmen. A couple at the back fell, screaming, but the rest ran on.

'Which direction?' Quinn called desperately to Thea, who was plunging ahead. 'Where are we going?'

Thea glanced back. 'Follow me,' she said, and began chanting again.

As Quinn watched, he saw sparkling light stretch out like an uneven, twisting carpet across the marshes. Her magic was showing them the safe way, Quinn realised.

Grimly, they hurried on. The cold and the mist seemed to close in around Quinn, turning his clothes damp and clammy. He hoped Thea's magic could lead them the right way.

A loud splash and a curse sounded behind

him. Quinn spun around as a great, black-armoured guardsman lumbered out of the marshes. His feet were sinking under him, but he was ploughing his way forward through sheer might. He held a huge double-handed sword before him and when he saw Quinn he roared and charged.

Quinn yelped and snatched for his own sword. His feet slipped as he did so, and the great sword sliced right over his head.

Quinn lunged, his light, golden blade taking the guardsman's legs out from under him and the man fell, hitting the brackish water with an almighty splash that sent a small wave washing over the grass. His heavy armour dragged him down.

Quinn scrambled to his feet, his golden sword held out before him. He didn't have time to turn and run. Two more Black Guards came charging out of the mist. Quinn backed away. The guardsmen took careful steps to the side, feeling their way on the uncertain surface as they tried to flank him. More Black Guards followed, emerging like dark ghosts along the path. Quinn held his sword out before him as he followed Thea's chanting.

'Keep going!' he yelled.

The two guardsmen lunged. Quinn swept up his sword and parried one, but the other charged full force towards him. The guardsman's shoulder caught Quinn full on his chest and the weight of the hard black armour sent him flying back. He collided with Thea and felt her fall too. Her chant broke off as she hit the ground.

Guardsmen threw themselves forward. Quinn rolled and a sword cut into the grass where he'd just been lying. Another guardsman stabbed down at him. Quinn blocked the blow just in time. He pushed with his heels. If it hadn't been for the treacherous footing, the guardsmen would have surrounded him by now.

Quinn swung his sword at ankle level, and the guardsmen leapt back. One lost his balance and disappeared into the water with a cry, but the others advanced in a line. Quinn felt Thea gain her feet behind him, but he didn't dare turn to flee. The guardsmen would cut him down the moment he turned his back.

There were seven guardsmen advancing on him now. Quinn managed to find his feet, but he had no idea how he was going to hold all of them off. He hadn't had any real training, and the marshes went on for miles. It would take all day to cross them, and only one guardsman had to get to him.

He clenched his teeth. *I'm not giving up!*

The guardsmen lifted their weapons.

'Run!' he shouted to Thea.

They sprinted, plunging into the mist as they skirted the guardsmen. Quinn heard a shout and a crash and someone splash into water, but the mist was swirling and he couldn't see anything. He leapt from grass tussock to grass tussock, desperately trying to find a good footing.

A small pond loomed up ahead, and Quinn took it at a flying leap. He hit the water and felt his legs sink down. He grabbed hold of solid ground and hauled himself up. He'd lost sight of Thea, but he couldn't go looking for her now.

He gained his feet and stumbled on.

Something hit him from the side with the force of a charging bull. Pain flared in his arm and shoulder and he was smashed to the ground, skidding over the mud and sodden grass. He wiped the globs of mud out of his eyes and stared up.

Clean and pristine, with a gleaming helmet and purple plumage sticking up, Lord Lorimer stood above him. A slimy smirk spread across his face, as he waved his sword above him.

'At last, boy,' he gloated, 'I have you.'

CHAPTER 15

A COLD EMBRACE

Quinn tried to rise, but agony shot through his whole body and he slumped back down.

'I have looked forward to this since the Emperor told me you hadn't drowned with your miserable parents,' Lorimer sneered. 'Now I will finish the job I started. Emperor Marek's blood-line ends here!'

'Not today,' Quinn spat.

He kicked out with all his might. His feet shot under Lorimer's shield and caught the man full on his armoured stomach. It knocked him staggering back, giving Quinn a chance to clamber to his feet. He ignored the knife-sharp pain all down his left arm and dragged his sword free.

Lorimer charged forward, swinging, and Quinn beat the man's sword down. He sent a backhand swipe at Lorimer's head, but Lorimer caught it on his shield. Quinn followed it up with a slash that almost took Lorimer's feet away from under him. The man jumped back just in time.

A faint gust of air cleared the mist just long enough for Quinn to see more Black Guard closing in, but Quinn didn't care. Lorimer was his enemy. The man had murdered his parents and had tried to kill him. He was the one who'd caused all the misery and unhappiness in Quinn's life. He'd stolen Quinn's parents from him and had let Vayn crush Alariss under his heels.

He hammered a blow at Lorimer's head and the man retreated again.

Quinn felt the anger building up in him once more, burning like a furnace, threatening to overcome him, and he sensed the dragonform inside stir in response.

No! He wasn't going to do this as a dragon.

He'd defeat Lorimer as himself. He'd show Lorimer what it was like to fight the true Emperor of the Twelve Islands face to face.

He launched another attack, blows whistling in at Lorimer from every side. Lorimer's shield spun from his arm as Quinn's attack cut it almost in half.

'You killed my parents!' Quinn bellowed, and for the first time, he saw fear in Lorimer's eyes.

Lorimer took his sword in both hands. With a scream, he launched an attack. Quinn stepped easily to one side and the sword stuck in the muddy grass. Quinn didn't give Lorimer time to recover his weapon. He slashed out and Lorimer staggered back, retreating faster and faster, his feet sending up splashes of black water. Quinn heard the shouts of guardsmen, but he didn't care.

Then, out of the corner of his eye, he saw a great, dark, looming figure with long arms and a heavy, blocky head appear from the mist. For a second he wondered if it was Ulric, using his shadow dragon powers, but the terrifying creature was all too real.

Lorimer saw the awe in Quinn's eyes and turned to look for himself. The creature let out a roar of anger, a cry of pure hate and malice. Vayn's magical creation knew nothing but rage – it didn't know the difference between Quinn and Lorimer and it certainly didn't care.

With another roar, it bumbled forward, tearing at them both.

Quinn leapt to the side, hacking at the creature with his sword. The metal tore off a chunk of stone that exploded into the air, but still it came forward. It flailed its fists in the air – yellow troll eyes burning with magical anger.

'See what you're up against,' Lorimer called. 'You'll never defeat Vayn!'

Quinn dodged once more. If he didn't get out of there, he'd be turned to stone.

Suddenly, he had a flash of inspiration. *Turned to stone . . .*

With a cry of anger, Quinn dodged past the troll and headed straight towards Lorimer's outstretched sword.

'You want to die by my sword, you worm?'

'You'll die before me, Lorimer,' Quinn cried.

As expected, the Stone Troll lumbered after Quinn as he sprinted towards Lorimer. As he approached, Quinn ducked, rolled away from the sword Lorimer had waiting, and skirted past him. With a kick to the lord's back, Quinn sent him straight into the troll's arms.

'No!' Lorimer yelled in terror, unable to stop himself.

The Stone Troll lumbered forward and grabbed Lorimer in a deathly embrace. He struggled for a moment, but then every movement in his body slowed. His skin darkened and stiffened. Life seemed to drain from his body. His eyes hardened. His eyelids froze mid-blink. His mouth stopped moving, stretched wide in a silenced scream. Slowly, his entire body turned to stone and he toppled sideways to lie, unmoving, in the marsh.

Quinn stared down at the man but felt no pity. If anyone had deserved this, it was Lorimer.

Around him, Quinn heard shouts of shock and fear. The Black Guard were retreating. Some of them were even fleeing, leaving their weapons and shields behind as they ran for the safety of Astria. Quinn stood, looking at his defeated opponent. He had beaten Lorimer, but it still didn't feel good. His parents were still dead.

Suddenly he snapped out of it, as more Stone Trolls lumbered out of the marshes. If he was turned to stone now, his friends would have no chance, and he'd never get to overthrow the man who had started all of this: Vayn.

As if just thinking about the Emperor was enough, magic flared in front of him, roaring up in burning, purple flames that seemed to snap like whips through the air. In the midst of them, Vayn's face appeared on the defeated Stone Troll's head.

'Who do you think you are, boy?' the Emperor raged. 'You are nothing! Your father was ten times more powerful than you, and I crushed him. You will never take my throne! I will grind you and your pathetic friends to dust! When I am finished with you, you will beg me to kill you.'

But Quinn wasn't listening. *His father!* That

was what Vayn had said. Marek had had power over the earth: stone, minerals, metals. If he pleased he could strengthen them with his magic to make the strongest of fortresses. Or, he could use his fiery breath to melt fierce armour or high walls. Maybe Quinn had the same power.

He let the anger surge up in him again, and this time he didn't push it back down. He rode it, letting it carry him forward, and his dragon-form came upon him, faster and easier than before. His body grew, his wings and tail burst out, and golden scales covered his body. His neck and head elongated, and in seconds he had transformed. Vayn's face on the Stone Troll twisted in hatred.

'Dragonblood!' Vayn spat.

Quinn flapped his wings, sending the mist eddying away, and lifted into the sky. He felt fire boil up inside him, and he kept it there, burning hotter and hotter until it raged like the sun in him. Then he bent his neck and sent a fireball shooting right at the Stone Troll.

Vayn shrieked, and his face disappeared. The

fireball caught the Stone Troll full on its chest, and the stone seemed to melt, flowing and dripping down, like it had been turned to hot rubber, sending steam hissing up from the water as molten stone splashed down. Then the Stone Troll slumped, falling to pieces as it dropped. In moments, only glowing lumps of rock showed where the monster had been.

Quinn let out a roar of triumph. *I was right! I do have my father's Earth Dragon powers!* He scanned the swamp, his keen eyes picking out the hulking forms of the Stone Trolls. Then he tucked in his wings and swooped towards them.

EPILOGUE

Thea and Quinn knelt in front of a stone figure in the misty marshes while Ignus, Ulric, Maria and Mother Onyx looked anxiously on. He'd tracked down and destroyed the Stone Trolls, but now he had another promise to fulfil.

Quinn could see the figure in front of them was a young woman, but it was hard to make out much of her features beneath the solid stone.

'It's going to work,' Thea whispered beside him. 'Trust me.'

Quinn did trust her. Her magic was more powerful than any he'd seen, except for Vayn's.

But turning stone to flesh didn't seem possible.

'I want you to concentrate,' Thea said. She held out a taper in front of him. 'I'm going to need Earth Dragon fire for this.'

He'd transformed into a dragon twice now, but this was something different. If he changed now, the fire he produced would fry Thea like an egg. Instead, he closed his eyes. He remembered the feel of the wind against his scales, the way his eyes could see every detail of the ground from high in the sky, the taste of the air and the vast strength in his wings. He gently blew on the taper.

'That's it,' Thea whispered.

The taper burst into life with a white-hot flame – bright enough to illuminate the marsh around them.

Quinn backed away, letting Mother Onyx come forward to take his place. She was carrying an elaborately crafted, hollow metal ball on the end of a chain that she'd unearthed from her magic shop. Quinn could sense the magical power invested in it and could smell the incense stuffed inside.

Carefully, Thea placed the taper inside the metal ball and shut the clasp. Moments later, the incense caught alight, and a faint trickle of smoke emerged from the ball.

Together, Thea and Mother Onyx began to chant, and Quinn felt Thea's powerful magic wrap around the ball. The spell kept building until Quinn felt it thrumming uncomfortably against his bones. At last, white smoke billowed out from it.

'Is it done?' Maria asked, sounding worried.

'The magic and the incense in combination with the dragon flame should reverse the petrification,' Thea said. 'The principle is simple, but the power Vayn gave to the Stone Trolls was immense.'

She took the ball from Mother Onyx and waved it back and forth in front of the stone figure of the woman until wreaths of smoke spread around it. Quinn stared, waiting to see what would happen.

Slowly, the grey stone began to fade, at first faintly, but then more visibly. At last Quinn could see pale skin and dark hair emerging. The hard eyes softened and became bright. With a gasp, the woman sucked in air.

Maria leapt forward with a cry. 'Anna!' She grabbed her cousin and embraced her tightly.

'Wh-what's going on?' Anna began, confused. 'Where am I?'

Maria was laughing and crying at the same time, too happy to explain. 'Where do I begin?'

Mother Onyx shook Thea's shoulders. 'You did it! Great magic skills!'

Thea smiled broadly and passed the gently smoking ball to the older woman. 'As long as you keep this burning, you'll be able to free the rest of the Stone Trolls' victims.'

'Thank you,' Mother Onyx said. 'You promised you would free us and bring back those who were lost, and you kept your promise. Now I can find my son. Keriss Island will not forget what any of you have done. I will make sure of it.' She turned to Quinn and gave him a bow. 'Keriss Island will stand behind you.'

Quinn cleared his throat awkwardly. He still

wasn't used to people treating him as anyone important.

'Thank you,' he said.

'Here.' Mother Onyx pressed a small book into Thea's hands. 'This spell book has been in my family for generations. It's far beyond my abilities, but I could never bring myself to sell it. Maybe it will help.'

Quinn pulled out his golden sword. Now he'd found out what had really happened to his parents, and recruited another Dragon Knight, it was time to get off the misty island.

He lifted the sword and peered into the blade. An image appeared, showing a gigantic, glittering golden dome, high up in the sky, with clouds racing swiftly past it.

'That's the Island of the Golden Sun,' Ulric said, looking over Quinn's shoulder.

Quinn reached down and picked up a backpack of supplies given to them by the townspeople. 'Then that's where we must go next . . .'

DRAGON
KNIGHTS

ULRIC THE SHADOW DRAGON

DRAGONFORM

An emerald green dragon, with a long body,
pointed face, curved horns and amber eyes.

BACKGROUND

Twelve years ago, in the days of Emperor Marek, Ulric
patrolled the Islands of Alariss, gathering information on
any threat to the empire. When Vayn outsmarted him and
launched an attack on the Imperial Castle, and the empire
fell, Ulric and the other knights fled to escape imprisonment
or death at the hands of the Black Guard.

OCCUPATION

Helping poor traders survive in the misty marshes of
Keriss by using his shadow abilities.

DRAGON KNIGHTS

ATTRIBUTES

Ulric is a playful and witty character, always quick with a witty comeback or a joke. His charm can sometimes seem like arrogance, but his usefulness and loyalty should never be in doubt.

STRENGTHS

Not only can Ulric fly and breathe fire, like the rest of the Dragon Knights, but he also has the power of shadow magic. Whether in his human or dragonform, this power enables him to confuse his enemies. By projecting shadow magic, he can make other people see things that aren't really there, which comes in handy when sneaking past patrols or taking on the Black Guards. Ulric can also use his power to cloak other people, as long as they're in close proximity to him.

WEAKNESSES

Shadow magic doesn't last forever. Eventually the mirages that Ulric weaves will wear off. If that happens at the wrong time, or in the wrong place, it can lead to a world of trouble.

DRAGON
KNIGHTS

**READ ON FOR MORE
DRAGON KNIGHTS ADVENTURES**

J. R. CASTLE

DRAGON
KNIGHTS

THE STORM DRAGON

CHAPTER I

THE GOLDEN SUN

The sun had sunk behind the mountains some time ago, but its afterglow still lit the western sky like the heat from a furnace. It seemed almost as if the distant Imperial Isle was on fire.

Quinn turned away and looked to the east. The dusk was spreading above scant pine trees and shadowed mountaintops. In less than an hour it would be fully dark. A rising wind ruffled his hair and stung his eyes. He shivered at its deep, cold bite and drew his cloak closer around him.

Winter had arrived sooner than expected. Out

here, on the exposed mountainside, they were at the weather's mercy. At least Ignus and Ulric had helped to get a campfire started before they set off to scout the area. That had been hours ago.

'Remind me again why we're up here instead of staying at an inn?' grumbled Thea. She huddled even closer to the flames, her long red hair almost dangling in them.

'Because of the amazing view,' Quinn said jokingly, and sat down. Seeing her scowl, he added, 'And because we're staying out of the way of Black Guard patrols.'

'What patrols? I haven't seen a single Black Guard since we got here!'

'Hmm,' Quinn murmured. Thea was right; it had been suspiciously quiet lately on the Black Guard front. 'Perhaps they're all tucked up cosy in their barracks, eating and drinking their way through our taxes.'

'Wishing you were still with them?' Thea asked, with a half-smile.

'Gods, no.'

The wind rose again, bringing a few dancing snowflakes with it. Quinn sucked air sharply through his teeth. 'Whoever called this island "The Golden Sun" must have been off his head on fermented wartberries. It's freezing!'

'I think you'll find that was the gods, Quinn. "A golden sun they set to the East of The Imperial Isle, and a silver moon to the West, that men might know their handiwork." Book of Makings, chapter one, verse six.'

'Never had you down for a religious type.'

Thea shrugged. 'I'm not. But it makes for a nice story.'

'Speaking of books, how are you getting on with the one Mother Onyx gave you?'

Thea brightened at once. She drew the slim black spell book from the folds of her clothes and held it open on her lap.

'It's going great! I've already mastered three of the major glyphs, and I'm nearly there with the Sassenava Incantation, though there's this one tricky bit where you have to sort of *hiccup*, because it's written in the Lost Speech of Eld and that's how you pronounce . . .' Her voice tailed off as Quinn held up a hand.

'The short version?' he asked.

'I can do more stuff.' Thea grinned. 'How about you? How's that dragonblood pumping?'

Quinn looked at the edges of his hand, where the light from the fire made his skin glow blood-red. *That's dragonblood in there.* It still hardly seemed real.

In the last few weeks he'd learned things about himself that he could never have imagined. He had dragonblood – the ability to shift his form into that of a dragon. As if that weren't enough, his dragonblood was royal. Quinn was the lost son of the Emperor and Empress.

His father, Emperor Marek, had been an Earth Dragon, giving him power over stones, minerals and metal. Quinn was sure he'd inherited the same power, and the way he'd melted a fearsome Stone Troll in the marshes on Keriss seemed to confirm it. He was capable of more, though, he knew it. So far he'd hardly had time to scratch the surface of his new powers.

'We should practise,' he told Thea. 'It'll kill some time while we wait for Ignus and Ulric.'

Thea glanced up at the thickening snowfall. 'Good idea. Maybe it'll take my mind off this filthy weather, too.'

Quinn rubbed his hands together until they tingled. Nearby was a boulder about the size of his head. That would do. He took a breath and began to concentrate.

'What are you doing?' Thea asked.

'Melting the rock!'

'What for?'

'Just watch,' Quinn muttered through gritted teeth.

He felt dragonblood power radiate from him, building between his hands and lashing out towards the rock. *Change,* he willed it. *Shift your form* . . .

Thea looked on as the rock warped and flexed before them. It was solid granite, but Quinn moulded it with his mind as if it were soft clay. He stretched the sides to produce two crude wings, made a head bulge from the front and tweaked a beak into place, then added two stubby little legs.

'It's a bird!' Thea laughed.

Quinn wiped sweat from his forehead. 'There. Not bad for a first try, huh?'

'Not bad at all. Now it's my turn. Let's see . . .' Thea leafed through her spell book until she found a page filled with runes that looked to Quinn like thorns and claws. She held the book open with one hand and gestured with the other. '*Verem, vita, aeolus!*'

The stone bird twitched. Its beak snapped. It gave a single hoarse croak and beat its wings as if it was trying to fly.

Thea wrinkled her nose, unsatisfied, and muttered something. Suddenly, silently, the bird floated up into the air. Thea's finger moved with it, as if joined by an invisible string.

Quinn clapped. 'Come on, little guy! You can do it!'

'I'm giving him some help,' Thea laughed. She raised her arm and the bird, still flapping awkwardly, rose into the snowy night sky above them.

As they watched the stone bird fly, without warning, the sky lit up. A curtain of seething blue light tore across their view from one end to the other. The clouds overhead shrank back.

Quinn jumped to his feet. Thea gasped. Her concentration broke. The stone bird, suddenly motionless, fell like a brick to shatter on the ground below.

'What *is* that?' Quinn asked in astonishment.

'The Seraphic Lights,' Thea breathed. 'Of course! This high in the mountains, you can see them clearly.'

Quinn looked in amazement at the rippling light show before them. He wasn't sure if they were magical or natural or some weird combination of both. There was beauty in the uncanny light, but yet Quinn felt dread stealing up inside him. Something evil was at hand. He could feel it in the air.

'Look!' He pointed to where ragged dark holes were appearing in the misty light above them.

No, not holes – *eyes*. Then a cruel slash of a mouth opened below. The image of a terrible face formed before them, hundreds of feet tall. A face he knew.

Quinn bared his teeth as a surge of hatred hit him. 'Vayn!'

The gigantic face laughed, and the laughter thundered down the mountainside, shaking the powdery snow loose. Quinn stood his ground, glaring back at the image of the Emperor: the usurper, the tyrant, the man who had murdered his parents.

'Little children, you are very far from home,' Vayn gloated. 'Do you think that your pitiful rebellion has a chance, now that you have released both Ulric and Ignus? Bravo. Two mighty Dragon Knights . . . a dullard and a rogue!'

Quinn drew a breath to shout defiance in Vayn's face, but Thea gripped his arm. 'Don't make a sound,' she hissed in his ear. 'You'll bring down an avalanche on top of us.'

Vayn's features twisted, no longer mocking,

but a demonic mask of fury. His voice rose to a shriek as he spoke. 'Heed me now! Crawl back to where you came from, little worms, and hide. Persist, and I warn you, my agents are everywhere. I will find you, and when I do, I will hang your ragged corpses from the palace walls as a warning to dragonblood filth and those who follow them!'

The curtain of light suddenly collapsed and flickered out, as if Vayn's rage was too much for it to bear.

Quinn and Thea stood, breathing hard, looking at one another.

'For the record,' said Thea with a nervous laugh, 'we're not going to take the "run away and hide" option, right?'

'You can if you like,' Quinn said. 'I'm going to free the rest of the Dragon Knights. And we're taking Vayn down.' He grabbed another lump of wood and threw it into the fire, hard. A shower of sparks went up. 'If that little show was meant to scare me, it didn't work.'

PICCADILLY PRESS

Thank you for choosing a Piccadilly Press book.

If you would like to know more about our authors, our books or if you'd just like to know what we're up to, you can find us online.

www.piccadillypress.co.uk

You can also find us on:

We hope to see you soon!